the
beautiful between

the
beautiful between

alyssa b. sheinmel

Alfred A. Knopf
New York

THIS IS A BORZOI BOOK PUBLISHED BY ALFRED A. KNOPF

Visit us on the Web! www.randomhouse.com/teens

Educators and librarians, for a variety of teaching tools, visit us at www.randomhouse.com/teachers

Library of Congress Cataloging-in-Publication Data
Sheinmel, Alyssa B.
The beautiful between / by Alyssa B. Sheinmel. — 1st ed.
p. cm.
Summary: Connelly Sternin feels like Rapunzel, locked away in her Upper East Side high-rise apartment studying for the SAT exams, until she develops an unlikely friendship with her high school's Prince Charming and begins to question some of the things that have always defined her life.
ISBN 978-0-375-86182-6 (trade) — ISBN 978-0-375-96182-3 (lib. bdg.) —
ISBN 978-0-375-89620-0 (e-book)
[1. Friendship—Fiction. 2. Fairy tales—Fiction. 3. New York (N.Y.)—Fiction.] I. Title.
PZ7.S54123Be 2010
[Fic]—dc22
2009022772

The text of this book is set in 11-point Bembo.

Printed in the United States of America
May 2010
10 9 8 7 6 5 4 3 2 1

First Edition

This book is for
Doris Dorr Sheinmel
and
Diane Liebson Buda

1

If you thought of high school as a kingdom—and I don't mean the regular kind of kingdom we have today, like England or Norway, I mean those small ones in fairy tales that probably weren't kingdoms at all so much as they were nobledoms where the nobles considered themselves kings and granted themselves the right of prima nochte, that kind of thing—if you thought of my high school like one of those, then Jeremy Cole would be the crown prince. The crown prince who could choose from all the women in his father's domain—and not only choose them but also have them parade in front of him at, say, a dance, trying to catch his eye, hoping to be chosen.

I don't know where I'd fall in the fairy-tale-kingdom hierarchy. I'm hardly Cinderella. I'm not beautiful and I'm not poor, and we have a cleaning lady who comes once a week, so I'm not stuck with the housework. Not Snow White either—the dwarfs always struck me as stranger than they were endearing, and wild animals don't look so much cute and cuddly to me as rabid and flea-ridden. Sleeping Beauty—not a chance. I'd be happy if I could just sleep through the night, let alone one hundred years. But I guess I could be Rapunzel; I do have long hair and I'm locked not so much in a tower by a wicked queen as in an Upper East Side apartment building by the SATs and college applications. Which are wicked enough for a hundred wicked queens and then some. Just my luck: Rapunzel, who wasn't a princess at all; Rapunzel, who—in at least some of the versions of the story—didn't have a happy ending.

It's pretty easy, sitting in the cafeteria, to imagine I'm in a fairy-tale kingdom, to transform the girls one by one from trendy students into stately-attired ladies. Just take the prettiest girl in the room, the most popular, whose clothes hang on her so lightly that you know she could pull off a gown as easily as she can those tight jeans with that black tank top. Give the boys swords hanging from their belts, and turn their baseball caps into crowns. I guess high school cafeterias are kind of like a royal court: your chance to show off the latest fashions, to make an entrance, and, if you're lucky, to be invited to have an audience before the royals—you know, sitting at the cool table.

I never sit at the cool table. I'm not at the nerds' table either, though I admit to having had a few dangerous weeks there in middle school when I was caught talking to myself in the stairwell. Now I know better, and keep my little reveries to myself.

Sometimes I grab a bagel and run off to the library to work on my SAT words, but mostly I just sit at the table right smack in the middle of the room, the biggest table, the one where almost anyone could sit and fit in just fine. So it's not that Jeremy's choosing me was a total shock because I was a dork. I mean, I am a dork, in my own "Hey, have you read this amazing novel?" kind of way—but not in any of the ways that get you kicked out of the kingdom. I speak up in class, but not too much; I come to school with my skirt too short and a black coffee in hand (even though I add so much sugar that you can barely taste the coffee); I even sneak out of the building between classes from time to time and stand on the corner with the smokers, bitching about the latest history substitute. The popular girls tolerate me just fine; the cool boys never take note.

So here I am, sitting at the central table in high court, staring at Alexis Bryant, who is sitting across from me and picking at a plate of limp lettuce. Alexis and I used to have playdates when we were younger, and the snacks at her house were always organic and whole-grain, while at my house, it was all Wonder bread and Coca-Cola. I wonder whether anyone else notices that Alexis is anorexic. Anorexia is so 1990s. In the twenty-first century, you only noticed when girls got skinny because they were doing a lot of blow. Even when celebrities got checked into clinics for eating disorders, rumors always flew that it was just a cover-up for their drug problems.

Emily Winters sits down next to me, her bangle bracelets clicking against themselves. She has to take them off when we're in class because they're so loud, but she always wears them in between classes, before and after school, and at lunch.

"Did you hear who Jeremy Cole is dating?"

Like anyone else would when Jeremy's name is mentioned, I snap to attention. "No, who?"

"Well, this is just a rumor, but I swear to God, I heard he hooked up with Beverly Edwards last weekend."

"No!"

"Yes!"

"But she's so . . . She's not smart. Once she asked Ms. Jewett whether *To Kill a Mockingbird* was a hunting book."

"She must have been joking."

"She wasn't."

"He can't be dating her."

"Maybe he just hooked up with her."

A new voice enters the conversation, a guy's voice all high-pitched and pretending to be girly: "We should take him out back and beat the crap out of him."

Emily and I look up—Jeremy is sitting on the other side of me. If my face is anything like Emily's, I'm blushing wildly. Emily pretends to be done eating and leaves me. Alone. With Jeremy Cole. I'm sure that everyone's watching; this table is right across from the food line, right smack in the center. Everyone can see.

"What's wrong, Sternin?" He grins at me.

I always liked the idea of being called by my last name but figured I didn't have the kind of name that adapted well to that. No one has ever called me Sternin before.

I guess because of that, I didn't respond right away. "Connelly?" Jeremy prompts.

"Yeah?" The magic of "Sternin" is gone, so I can be nonchalant.

"I hear you're having trouble in physics."

"Where'd you hear that? I'm doing fine. I'm fine."

It feels like the chatter in the cafeteria has gone quiet and everyone is listening to us. Which, by the way, isn't entirely beyond reality, because people are always watching Jeremy Cole.

"Hey, don't worry." Jeremy seems surprised. I realize that my response had been pretty shrill.

"Well, then why are you mentioning it?" I ask, still defensive.

"Okay, so I didn't so much hear it as I did see your test score when Mr. Kreel gave them out." I must look horrified, because he adds, "It wasn't on purpose, Connelly, it was just that you were sitting right in front of me."

Does Jeremy know that physics is already—a month into the school year!—my lowest grade this semester and I'm freaking out because one bad grade can bring your whole GPA down and then it's goodbye, Columbia, the school you've been working your whole life to get into? I'm angry at him. How dare he come over here with his preternaturally perfect tan and his charmingly gap-toothed smile and announce my shitty grade. Why would a person do that? It's just mean.

"Look," I say defensively, pushing my hair behind my ears and then back out again, "I'm going to work on it. I'll figure it out."

"Hey—calm down. I'm sorry." Jeremy touches my arm. "Sternin, really." And I melt because he's calling me Sternin again. His hand on my arm doesn't hurt his case either. I can actually feel the little hairs tingling. "I was just going to offer to help."

"Huh?" I say dumbly.

"I'm really good at physics. You seemed so bummed about your grade. I could help you with that lab that's due next week—it would bring your grade up to at least a B if you did well."

Oh thank God. I wanted to hire a physics tutor, but I didn't want to have to admit to my mom that I was having this much trouble. And Jeremy might be cheap enough that I could pay for him myself, without my mom's help. Maybe he sees it as one of his princely duties to help a citizen in distress, and paying him would be like paying taxes.

"I could pay you cash, but it depends on how much—I mean, I can't afford much."

Jeremy laughs. "Dude, I didn't mean you had to pay me. I just wanted to help you."

"Oh." I'm suspicious again, because I can't think of why Jeremy Cole would want to help me.

"Yeah, you could pay me in kind. I could use some help with my SAT words."

"Couldn't you just get a real tutor for that?" I ask dumbly.

Why am I trying to talk him out of hanging out with me? Shut up, Connelly, shut up. Let Jeremy do the talking.

"I've tried that. I still suck. Maybe you can teach me something they couldn't."

Either Jeremy is hitting on me and is remarkably smooth—only the savviest of men would know that complimenting my vocabulary is the best way to get on my good side—or he's genuine. Either way, I'm pretty much jelly by now.

"Okay, sounds good."

"Thursday after school?"

"Okay."

"Meet you in the lobby."

"Okay."

"All right, Sternin, stay cool."

How is it that Jeremy makes me feel like I'm twelve and he's twenty?

2

My mom isn't entirely unlike the evil stepmother in "Cinderella." I don't mean that she's wicked—she's a perfectly nice person and mother. But I think she would love to be part of a more glamorous world than the one that she inhabits, and sometimes I think she's hoping that her daughter will get her there. I can't explain why; maybe it's because she's sent me to the school I go to, Jeremy Cole's school, a school where celebrities' children go—that kind of place. She's always made sure I wear the right clothes; shopping is one of the few ways we really spend time together.

These days, just like the wicked stepmother who wanted her daughters to marry the prince so that she could rub shoulders with the royals, my mother seems to be waiting for me to come home with a nice high-society boy through whose parents she could catch a peek at the best of New York. I know that I can always get her attention if I have some good gossip from school about something that's going on in some family whose name she knows. She loves any kind of gossip about people like that.

So you can imagine her delight when I walk in with Jeremy Cole on Thursday afternoon. She certainly knows who Jeremy is—

his family is one of the wealthiest in New York. He's one of those boys you see pictured occasionally in *New York* magazine, whose family parties make it onto Page Six of the *Post*.

"Hey, Mom!" I call out as I open the door. I forgot to tell her Jeremy was coming over, and there's a possibility she's puttering around the apartment in an oversized T-shirt and rollers. It's not that she doesn't do stuff during the day—she goes to lunches, is on a charitable board or two—but every so often, she's just *here*. I wonder if she gets bored.

"Hey, honey," she responds, and comes out from her room in—phew!—jeans and a loose black T-shirt. Not quite what I imagine Jeremy's mom wears around the house, but nothing embarrassing either.

"Mom, this is Jeremy Cole."

When she talks to him, her voice is high-pitched. I can't tell if she's trying to sound fancy, or if she's nervous to be talking to him.

"Why, hello, Jeremy. I'm Ellen, Connelly's mother. She didn't mention she was bringing anyone over today."

"Nice to meet you, Mrs. Sternin." Jeremy replies robotically but politely, like a well-raised royal should.

"Oh, call me Ellen, please!" She laughs like "Mrs. Sternin" is preposterous, and her hand lands on Jeremy's upper arm. If we stay here, my mom will start to flirt—on my behalf, perhaps, but flirt nonetheless.

"Well, Mom, Jeremy and I have to study now, so we'll be in the other room." I head toward my bedroom, and Jeremy follows.

"All right, kids, let me know if you need anything. I could make you a snack or something."

My mother didn't even make me after-school snacks when I was in kindergarten.

❋ ❋ ❋

I open the door, and it isn't until Jeremy follows me inside that I realize that in my haste to get him away from my mother, I've brought Jeremy into my room. This is problematic on several levels. One, Jeremy may get the wrong idea. Two, my room is immaculate, and what if he messes with my stuff? Three, the dining room table would have been much more conducive to studying.

Alone with Jeremy Cole, I'm not quite sure what to do. I can't quite wrap my head around the fact that I went from barely ever having spoken to Jeremy Cole to having him here in my room. The weather today is humid and thick, even though it's October, and normally I'd check up on my books, because I'm protective of them and humidity curls the pages. But I can't possibly check on my books in front of Jeremy. He'll think I'm a freak.

Much to my relief, Jeremy takes the lead. He settles on the floor, leans against my bed, reaches into his bag, and pulls out his physics book. I'm a little embarrassed, looking around the room at the white wicker furniture that seemed so pretty when I was nine and looks so babyish now. I'm sure that there's nothing in Jeremy's room more than a year or two old, that everything is trendy and cool and up-to-date.

"All right, Sternin." He grins up at me. "An hour of Einstein, and then you gotta tell me what the hell 'defenestrate' means."

❋ ❋ ❋

Jeremy has a little sister. She's in seventh grade, but unlike most twelve-year-olds, she seems to have entirely skipped that preteen awkward phase. She's beautiful, with long, wavy blond hair—just the kind of hair a princess should have, the polar opposite of my stick-straight brown mess. Her name is Kate and everyone loves her, especially Jeremy.

After lunch today, buoyed by the knowledge that I was studying with Jeremy tonight, I invited Kate into the elevator. Only juniors and seniors are allowed to use the elevators, despite the fact that our school is ten stories high, being, as it is, smack in the middle of Manhattan, where buildings tend to go up more than they go out. The younger students get into trouble if they get caught taking the elevator, but the juniors and seniors always try to sneak them on. If we get caught, we pretend it was an accident—we were talking with them, helping them with homework, so they just followed us into the elevator. We didn't even realize.

I was waiting for the elevator when I saw Kate coming out of the nurse's office—the perfect excuse to offer her a ride.

"Hey, I'm heading up to the tenth floor—want a ride?"

Kate grinned at me. "Definitely!" She seemed energized by the offer, and practically skipped toward me and the opening elevator doors.

"What'll we say if Mrs. Turley catches us?" Mrs. Turley is the strictest teacher in the school.

"We'll say it was all my fault. I lured you in here with promises of a trouble-free flight up, with ice cream sundaes and elevator passes waiting for you at the top."

I've never felt so clever; certainly this is as much as I've ever said to Kate Cole.

"That's not fair," she said, stopping just before stepping into the elevator. "You shouldn't get in trouble for doing something nice."

No wonder everyone loves that girl. She even managed to say that without sounding like a goody two-shoes.

"Don't worry." I grabbed her arm and pulled her in. "The teachers love me. This is probably the naughtiest thing I've ever done."

She grinned at me again. "Yeah, but you're hanging out with Jeremy later; he'll get you into plenty of trouble before long."

I could feel myself blushing as the elevator ascended. Kate probably knew better than I why Jeremy had decided to help me with physics. I didn't know what to say to her; suddenly the ride up to the tenth floor seemed interminably long, and inviting Kate into the elevator seemed like a ridiculously bad idea. But then Kate just started giggling, and so did I, all the way up to the tenth floor.

"Don't worry, Connelly," Kate said as she headed to her class and I turned toward mine, "Jeremy may be the most popular boy in school, but he's really just as dorky as you and me."

And then she grinned at me, and I smiled back. I don't believe for a second that Kate Cole is a dork, let alone Jeremy, but it still made me feel better knowing that she thinks they are—and that she thinks we're the same.

Now, in the two hours we spend studying, Kate calls Jeremy's cell phone twice, and after both calls Jeremy talks about her for a good ten minutes. He tells me she's the family mascot. He calls her Mouse when he talks to her on the telephone. When she hears me saying "Hi, Kate" in the background, Jeremy tells me, she says,

"Oooh, Connelly Sternin is super pretty," and I'm happy for the rest of the evening, because maybe that means that I'm one of the juniors that the middle schoolers look up to.

We spend a lot more time on physics than we do on vocabulary, so I think I'm getting the better end of the studying deal. Then again, when Jeremy leaves, he says, "Better abscond." So he's learned at least one new word, while I don't feel any closer to understanding vector equations.

❀ ❀ ❀

I look for Kate at school the next day. I want to say hi to the girl who called me pretty. Kate isn't the kind of kid who's intimidated by upperclassmen; she hangs out with the juniors all the time. She's the only seventh grader—the only kid from any of the other grades—who regularly spends time in the junior lounge. Anyone else's sister and everyone would complain, but no one would ever say anything to Jeremy. And Kate's so cool that no one minds anyway.

At lunch, Jeremy sits next to me again, and we spend the better part of the period staring at Alexis Bryant cutting her single lettuce leaf into perfect little squares—sixteen, we count—and then eating them one at a time. I think Jeremy had every intention of talking to me when he sat down, but instead, neither of us can tear our eyes away from Alexis. She seems to enjoy the attention. Jeremy and I don't say anything, but it's obvious that she knows we're watching. She looks smug.

When she finally gets up, Jeremy and I turn to face each other. The teachers' table is right behind this one, and I find myself staring at the backs of their heads. How is it that none of them notice—

or that they all turn a blind eye? I'm not entirely sure where the teachers fall in the fairy-tale-kingdom hierarchy—everything I can think of is too mean, too much like calling them servants. I rack my brain for the right title for them. Jeremy's voice interrupts my thoughts.

"Jesus. That girl is so fucked-up."

"I know. What's more fucked-up is that we couldn't take our eyes off her," I say, and Jeremy looks guilty. "I don't mean it was our fault—I just mean we couldn't look away, you know, like the pull to look at a car wreck." He looks really upset that I called us out for staring at her. "Jeremy, I'm sorry." He doesn't look at me. "Jer?" I say.

"Whatever. Sorry. It's just, I've seen someone who can't eat more than that, you know. And she really wanted to."

I try not to show my confusion. I glance around the lunch-room as though the crowd by the soda machine might give me some clue. Our school has a rule that you're not allowed to bring your own lunch—you have to eat the lunch that's served. I mean, I guess you could bring something in, but meals are built into the tuition, so you pay for the food whether you want to or not. Emily Winters and I did the math once, and it ended up being something like eleven dollars a day just for lunch, which seemed exorbitant to us. There are lots of choices, almost all the stuff you could have brought from home: plenty of stuff to make a salad or a sandwich out of, plus whatever the hot meal of the day is, and this is the only school I know of where even the pickiest of girls will eat the hot food—that's how good it is.

Alexis is proof, though, that being forced to eat the food the school makes has nothing to do with being forced to eat in general; the cafeteria staff don't notice or care what you put onto the trays emblazoned with the school's crest, which has been the same since it opened one hundred years ago. Back then it was an all-girls boarding school, with something like thirty students being trained in etiquette, piano playing, and occasionally literature. Now it's gained a reputation as one of the most academically rigorous schools in the city, known particularly for how much the girls excel at math and science. I wonder how the school's founders would feel about that, or about the way that girls and boys spill hungrily into the lunchroom now, heaping food on their trays and holding their forks in the wrong hand.

Jeremy doesn't seem to notice the silence that followed his comment, so I decide to change the subject. "Hey," I say brightly, "I've been looking for Kate all day. Wanted to say hi, but haven't been able to find her."

I remember that she was in the nurse's office the day before. "Is she home sick?" I ask.

Jeremy looks right at me then. "Yeah, she's home sick. I gotta go to class," he says, and starts getting up, so I do too, even though I have a free period after lunch.

"Okay," I say, feeling awkward. I mean, it's weird—he sits down next to me, and then we spend forty minutes watching an anorexic girl eat her lettuce-lunch, and then, as soon as we actually begin talking to each other, he's scrambling away. Clearly he's only interested in me for my vocabulary. Clearly he doesn't actually want to be my friend. Even if his sister thinks I'm super pretty.

"Studying on Monday?" he asks, resting his hand on the back of my chair.

"Huh?" I turn to face him, distracted by his long fingers so close to my shoulder.

He grins at me and I melt, like always. "Monday, Sternin? After school? There's that physics quiz on Tuesday. Gotta get you ready."

"Yeah, definitely." I say it too fast; I'm so excited that we're still studying together. I try to slow down. "Sounds good."

"Have a good weekend."

"You too. Hey—tell your sister I hope she's feeling better."

He shrugs. "Sick or not, Mouse is pretty happy to have an excuse to get out of her French test." He grins, and as he walks away, it seems to me that people part to make room for him to pass. Just like in Tudor England, where when the king's presence was announced, everyone had to give him the right-of-way.

✽ ✽ ✽

I spend the weekend alternating between studying for physics and the SATs. The physics is so hard that I've begun to consider the SATs a break. Emily Winters calls to quiz SAT words with me, but her phone calls irritate me, because they're interrupting my studying and I have my own rhythm. She invites me over to study with her, but I turn her down. I much prefer to be in my room. Even though it's not hot out, I have the air-conditioning turned up as high as it can go and I'm curled up on the bed, layers of blankets over me. I like to think that it's so cold, I can almost see my breath. I like to bury myself under blankets.

Maybe Emily only invites me because she knows I'm good at

the vocab and thinks I can help. I say no because I think studying alone is better. But then I remember how well studying with Jeremy went, that I did exactly what Emily is asking me to do with him and it wasn't at all counterproductive. I even learned a new word or two. Plus, it was fun.

I think about calling Emily back, about going over to her house and quizzing words back and forth over a box of pizza like they do on TV or in the movies. But I'm in my pajamas and my bed is so soft, and going all the way to her apartment seems like such a chore.

My mother pops her head in a few times, wishing me luck, asking if I'm hungry. Sometimes I think she wonders how I can stand to stay in all day, in bed, studying. My mom likes movement; she's almost never home during the day on weekends. She goes out shopping, meets friends for lunches, takes long walks around the city. When I'm not studying, sometimes I go with her. When I was little, I almost always went along—we rarely used a babysitter, and I was too young to be left alone. I felt very grown-up at lunch with her friends, at restaurants where I was the only kid. I still remember the feel of my legs swinging down from the chair. My mother used to complain that I was kicking her, which always confused me, since I thought I was hitting the table legs.

Mostly, I'd sit quietly at these lunches and watch; I knew I wasn't supposed to participate. You can learn a lot if you watch. Most of my mother's friends were married. They were women with whom my mother had gone to college; women who had been at—or maybe, come to think of it, in—her wedding; women who had known her as a wife. I'd watch the rings that flashed on their fingers and wonder why my mother, for all her stylishness, never wore jewelry. They discussed problems they thought I was too young to understand—fights with their husbands, impatience with their children. Maybe they thought I wasn't listening; I was given crayons and drew on paper placed over the tablecloth: princes and princesses and the castles they lived in. My mother's friends always looked to her for advice. No matter that she didn't have a husband—they wanted her ideas on how to liven up a quiet marriage; how to confront a husband who was overworking, overeating, even sleeping around. I might not have known the mechanics of what they were discussing, but I could tell that it was important and very, very grown-up.

My mother was always the prettiest woman at these lunches; none of the others could ever compare to her, with her dark hair, her painted nails, her bright lipstick, her fitted clothes. They always looked older than she did—even now, when I see her friends, I can never believe that my mother is the same age. I imagined she had a magic potion some fairy had given her, something that kept her looking young while the women around her aged. I didn't believe I would grow up to be as pretty as her; I don't look anything like her. I don't remember when I stopped accompanying her to these lunches. It's only now that I realize that I was the only kid there because the other women had husbands to leave their children with.

❊ ❊ ❊

I'm in the kitchen when I hear the front door swing open and closed. I'm eating cereal over the kitchen counter, even though it's three in the afternoon. I haven't bothered to turn the lights on, so the countertops look gray and dusty, even though our housekeeper just came a few days ago; when the lights are on, you can see that they're gleaming white.

"Hi, honey."

"Hey."

"How's studying going?"

"It's fine."

"Good." She's not really looking at me, she's sorting the mail. I wonder if she even remembers that I struggle with physics.

"Well, I'm going to go take a bath," she says. "I'll be out for dinner." She looks around the kitchen, as though it's just occurred to her that there might not be food enough for my dinner. "I'll leave some money in the drawer for you?"

"Okay, thanks."

"Okay, sweetie," she says, and heads for her room. I wonder whether having a roommate in college will be like this. Our conversation has been just long enough for my cereal to get soggy. I throw what's left in the garbage; it'll be dinnertime soon anyway.

3

On Monday, I bring my lunch from the cafeteria to the junior lounge so that I can work on physics. I really should be using my free time to study, though I did take the time to notice that Jeremy wasn't in the lunchroom before I decided to come up here. The lounge is completely empty, and more comfortable than studying in the library, since I can stretch out on the couches. I want to get some work done now so Jeremy doesn't think I'm a complete idiot when he comes over later. Between bites of a bagel and vector calculations, I see that Kate has wandered in.

"Hey, Connelly," she says, slipping her backpack onto the floor and perching on the couch across from me. "Have you seen Jeremy?"

I shake my head and pull myself into a sitting position. "Nope. He isn't in the lunchroom?"

"I didn't see him there. He must have gone out for a cigarette or something."

"Do you need him for something? I can go try to find him." The underclassmen aren't allowed to go out during lunch and free periods, and even I know where Jeremy and his friends go to smoke. There's a courtyard between a couple of apartment buildings around the corner. Even the teachers know about it, but they don't care enough to catch anyone in the act.

"It's okay."

"I didn't know Jeremy smoked," I say, trying to make conversation. Kate's being here is a nice break from studying.

"Yeah." She wrinkles her nose. "Makes him smell bad."

"Yeah."

Kate leans back against the couch, closing her eyes for a second. She looks tired. She opens her eyes and sees my books. "Physics, huh? I never understand it when my dad and Jeremy talk about it. It sounds so hard."

"Yeah, well, I'm sure they'll tutor you if you need it in a few years."

"Yeah, we'll see," she says, like she doesn't really believe it.

"I mean, if Jeremy has the patience to tutor me, he can tutor anyone."

Kate smiles at me. "He likes tutoring you, Connelly. He told me."

"I still can't figure out why he offered—I mean, he could be doing any number of more interesting things than helping a girl like me with physics."

I can't believe I just said that. I've been thinking it for days, but I can't believe I said it out loud. She'll think I'm trying to get her to tell me why her brother is suddenly interested in my physics grade. She probably knows everything about Jeremy.

"He just thinks you're cool. He told me."

"He thinks I'm cool?" The words are out of my mouth before

I can stop them. I can hear how excited I sound. Kate must think I'm ridiculously lame.

But she grins at me. "Yeah. I mean, you are."

It's such a nice compliment that I can feel my cheeks getting hot; I'm blushing.

"I thought you said we were dorks."

Kate shrugs. "Who says we can't be both?"

That makes me smile so wide that my mouth will hurt by the beginning of next period. Kate gets up to leave, and I tell her I'll let Jeremy know she was looking for him, and she says it's no big deal, she'll find him later, but thanks anyway, and good luck on the quiz.

Okay, I know Kate is four years younger than I am, but she sure seems a lot wiser. But then, someone like Kate wouldn't have to wonder why someone like her brother was taking an interest in her. Boys like that will probably always be interested in Kate.

❋ ❋ ❋

Later that afternoon, I'm freaking out because there's no way I'm going to pass the quiz tomorrow. None of the studying I've done has made a dent. Somewhere between neutrons and panic, there's Jeremy, leaning against my bed, calmly explaining to me that protons are positive and electrons are negative, and there's no air resistance in a vacuum, and it's just like math.

"That does not help. I hate math." My heart is actually racing. I'm terrified about taking this quiz. "I feel so stupid."

"Don't worry about it. I'm only good at this because my father's a science geek."

"Oh?" I remember that Kate said Jeremy and his dad talk about physics sometimes.

"Yeah, by the age of eight I already knew about atoms and quarks. He used to sneak into my room when my mom thought I was sleeping and give me science lessons. I thought dust particles were molecules until I was eleven."

I smile helplessly. "So I'm at a genetic disadvantage, is what you're telling me."

"I'm afraid so."

It's quiet for a minute, and when I bend over my notes again, Jeremy says, "Hey, Connelly, I didn't mean anything by that."

"By what?"

"About my father, I mean. I wasn't . . . That was insensitive of me, I'm sorry."

It takes me a second to realize he means because I don't have a father, it was insensitive of him to talk about his. Why bring that up? It's not like I went all sad the minute he mentioned his father. And anyway, as far as Jeremy knows, I'm just a girl whose parents are divorced. That's not so sad.

"What do you mean?"

"I mean"—he looks visibly uncomfortable—"I mean, your dad passed away. . . . I shouldn't be making fun of you for not having a dad to go over physics with you."

Now my heart is racing again, and it has nothing to do with math. Curiosity makes my muscles twitch. "How do you know about my dad?"

Jeremy looks taken aback. "What? I just—you know, people talk."

"Who?" I ask, suddenly accusatory. "Who talks? I don't talk."
I press my fingers into the floor as though I'm about to push myself up to stand. The hardwood floor suddenly feels hot under my hands.

"Who told you about my dad?" I ask again.

Jeremy's face looks like what I imagine mine does when faced with vector equations. I don't know what to do. I want to be angry at him, but now I feel guilty because I've made him look like that. I want to forget that this has happened. I don't want Jeremy to know how curious he's made me: How does he know about my dad? And what does he know?

"Hey, I'm sorry," I say. "Forget it. People talk, whatever. Let's switch to vocab so I can feel smart for a while."

Jeremy's face relaxes and he smiles slowly, like he's being careful about returning to his usual self. "All right, Sternin, but I'm not leaving until you're set for the quiz."

"Whatever, dude. Define 'peripatetic.'"

Even princes don't know everything.

4

I have trouble calming down after Jeremy leaves, and not just because I'm sure I'm still totally unprepared for the physics quiz. My
skin feels itchy, but not like I have to scratch it; it itches every time
I'm still—when I get into bed and try to read, when I turn out the
light and try to sleep. I'm thinking about my father, someone I
never knew. Or anyway, I have no memory of knowing him, so
that's the same thing.

This is what I do know, and it's strange to think this, because
I've never felt the need to lay it out before. He died just after I
turned two, and that's young enough that you can't really speak yet,
and I read somewhere that you can't build memories before you
have the language to express them. I don't remember living with
him, but I know that before my dad died, we lived in a townhouse
a few blocks east and south of here. But I can't remember the house,
or the way the furniture was laid out, or the smell of the carpet on
which I took my very first steps. And I don't know how my father
died. It's always been kind of hazy to me. When I was very young,
I had this notion of a man falling off a ladder, but I know that's
something I made up, a child's idea of how a person dies, maybe
something out of a movie I'd seen.

After my father died, we moved in with my grandmother—my mother's mother, who lives across town, on the Upper West Side. Her apartment was definitely not decorated with kids in mind. Everything is white and spotlessly clean. The apartment would be pristine but for my grandmother's complete inability to throw things away. I think I get that from her—the need to keep things, paired with a compulsion to make things neat no matter how cluttered. I like knowing that—being sure that I got something from her. There must be things I got from my father, things I will never be able to pinpoint.

We moved to this apartment the summer I turned eight, and I started a new school. My school, Jeremy's school, the one I still go to. It has kids from kindergarten through twelfth grade, and if you stay there all thirteen years, you get a special picture in the yearbook marked with the word "survivor." I still remember the first day of third grade: I saw Emily Winters with her mother and father; Alexis Bryant's mother and father, and her big sister leading her by the hand; even the Coles turned out, Jeremy's mother holding Kate's hand—she was still too young to go to our school. My mother held my hand tightly, but I don't think I even looked at her. I was looking at everyone else.

It was the first time I felt that I was missing something the other kids all had. For the first time, I could see that we were different, that there was something weird about me, something strange about my not having a father. And for the first time, it made me wonder—that same skin-itching, can't-be-still sensation I feel now. I didn't even realize yet that most kids had never lived with their grandparents. My mother and I used to curl up in her bed at Grandma's and watch TV and eat ice cream until I fell asleep. I always woke up in my room; I guess she'd carry me there once I was sleeping. My grandmother disapproved; she thought my mother was babying me, that I was getting too old to cuddle like that. I never heard her say anything about it; I could just tell by the look on her face when she walked past my mother's open door and saw us together. Now I assume she was silent because she felt sorry for us: her daughter, the widow, and her granddaughter, the half orphan.

I did not like this apartment when I saw it for the first time. At my grandmother's apartment, my mother's and my bedrooms were right next to each other. We shared a wall, so from my room, even with the door closed, I could hear Mom moving around; hear her voice on the phone, her radio in the background when she read. This apartment is laid out completely differently, with two bedrooms on opposite ends, each with its own bathroom. The kitchen and living room are in the middle, with an alcove for a dining room in between. It is an apartment for two people to be separated in. I didn't like it. But my mother was so excited the day we moved in, I knew better than to say anything. My grandmother had helped her pick the apartment out. Maybe she thought its layout seemed good for a single woman and her child: we'd each have so much privacy. My grandmother's cleaning lady was there to help us unpack; she still comes here once a week and uses the same cleaning products she uses at my grandmother's, so our apartments smell the same. The day we moved in was the first time I was aware that my mother and I felt differently about the same thing: I was sad and she was excited. "You'll be so close to your new school," she said, squeezing my shoulders.

The afternoon after my first day of third grade, my mother came to pick me up. I'd calmed down, having mostly forgotten about what I'd seen that morning. Everyone else was picked up by their mothers too, or, if their mothers worked, by a nanny. But after we got home, after I'd watched TV and paged through the chapter book the teacher had promised we'd read soon, I began to have the same sensation that had gripped me that morning. There was something about me that was different—something I didn't quite understand, something that made me nervous. The pages of the book seemed to stick together, and the words looked so big, and it seemed impossible that I would ever know what the letters meant when they were strung together. And I was a good reader—I'd been reading books more difficult than this all summer. I didn't want to face the next morning at school, because what if the next morning, all the fathers would be there again and I'd have to be different again.

I had to tell my mother why I couldn't go back. So I slid off my bed and walked across the apartment toward my mother's bedroom. I still wasn't used to what a long walk it was; we'd only been living here a couple of weeks. My mother's door was closed, but I opened it without knocking; I'd never had to be bashful about going into Mom's room at Grandma's house. The lights were out and Mom was lying on her side, turned away from me. But she was above the covers and fully dressed, so I supposed she was awake.

"Mommy?"

She rolled over and flicked on the light next to the bed. Her eyes were very red, and her hair was frizzled.

"What's the matter, sweetheart?"

I climbed onto the bed and snuggled next to her. She still wears the same perfume. Sometimes, when I smell it, it takes me right back to her bed, to the pillowcases that smelled like her.

"I don't want to go back to school tomorrow."

Her face became alert, and I was relieved. I was worried that she'd tell me I had to go, but instead she looked genuinely concerned, like this was a grown-up problem.

"Did someone say something mean to you? Did the teacher say something?"

"No." Why would my nice new teacher have said anything?

I could feel her body relaxing next to mine; could feel her arms around me becoming less stiff, her fingers loosening their grip on me. She brushed the hair out of my face. "Then what's the matter, sweetheart?" And now it didn't sound like she thought my problem was grown-up enough. I tried to explain.

"I'm different from the other kids."

"Everybody's different, sweetie," she said, and even at that age, I knew she was patronizing me. I had to make her understand that I couldn't go back.

"How come we don't have a daddy like everyone else?" I knew, by then, that my father was dead and what it meant to be dead, but that didn't explain why I didn't have a father.

My mother's arms became stiff again. Her face went white, and her hands held my arms so tight that it hurt—later I would see red marks where her fingernails had been. I don't think she meant to hurt me; I don't think she had control over her muscles at that moment.

I was terrified. My question had upset my mother like nothing I'd ever done. Worse than when I spilled cranberry juice on the sofa; worse than when I had knots in my hair that she had to untangle. She didn't say anything, and all I wanted was to undo what I'd done.

So, in my infinite eight-year-old wisdom, I said, "It doesn't matter, Mommy. I know it doesn't matter. I'll go back tomorrow. I promise."

And this seemed to work. Her body relaxed, but not completely. I could feel the tension still in her muscles, like she was nervous, anxious, that I might ask again, even if it wouldn't be for a very long time.

I left her room and went back to my book. That night, I fell asleep in my own bed. The next day, when she dropped me off, I let go of her hand and walked right into the school by myself, past the kids who were crying because they didn't want to leave their moms, past the moms who were hugging their kids tight because their kids didn't want to be left. I didn't want my mom to worry about me. I would turn off whatever was inside me that made me wonder why we were different.

After that, my mother always walked me to school and always came to pick me up, and I always dropped her hand and went right in, and then came out and took her hand for the walk home later—exactly like the other kids I watched so closely. I believed I could keep her calm, could make her happy. I didn't ever want to talk about my father again, and I didn't ever want to feel that skin-itching curiosity over him again. If I could just make myself be normal, then there would be nothing to wonder about. I just had to figure out a way how.

And then, one day, Emily Winters came into school and told

me that her parents were getting divorced. She said the word loudly, almost proudly, because it was a big grown-up word with all kinds of big grown-up implications.

I tried not to smile; I knew I shouldn't smile at Emily's very serious grown-up news. But I was excited, because here was the normalcy I'd been looking for. Lots of kids had divorced parents—there were two boys in our class whose parents were divorced, and at least three kids in the other third-grade class. This was a new school—no one here knew us from before, no one here knew my dad was dead. So I decided to lie.

"You know," I said, "that makes us the only divorced girls in Mrs. Focious's class."

Emily seemed to think I was an expert on divorce. I told her my father left when I was only two, that I barely remembered him. No need to be curious anymore: now I was an expert; now there was nothing I didn't know, because I got to make it up as I went along.

Emily said her father was moving to Chicago, but she'd still get to see him all the time. "He's getting a big house with an extra room in it just for me. And he promises that he's still going to visit all the time—he'll even still pick me up from school sometimes."

"That's great," I said wisely. My father had to be even farther away than Chicago, somewhere I couldn't get to—far enough that it would make sense that I never saw him, that he never visited. It had to be another country. Europe was too cool, a place the lucky kids got taken to on vacation. I thought of South America, but that was too strange, too exotic; there'd be too many questions.

"My dad lives in Arizona," I said, the lie rising easily in my throat.

"I'm actually really lucky," Emily continued. "My parents are getting joint custody." She said the new words slowly, as if they were big in her mouth. "My brother says that there's a girl in his class who never sees her father, because her parents hated each other so much, they never wanted to have to see each other again."

I jumped at the explanation. "That's like my parents. I haven't seen my dad once since he left."

"Wow," Emily said, her eyes growing wide. "That's really bad."

"Yeah," I said, proud of myself for the lie, happy to be like the girl in her brother's class. "But I'm used to it. It's always just been me and my mom."

Emily and I walked around holding hands for the rest of the day. When I got home, I almost told my mother about the lie. But my mother didn't believe in lying; she'd told me a thousand times that good girls didn't lie. So I didn't tell her, even though I wanted her to know that I'd found the one lie that I was sure was allowed, the one lie that would make everything okay.

But, even though I never asked about my father again, things still weren't the same. On the nights when I would go into her room to watch TV, my mother didn't hold me like she used to, and we each got our own bowl of ice cream. When I turned nine, she bought a TV for my bedroom, so our nights of TV and ice cream became much fewer and further between. I knew if I said anything to her, it would just bring her back to that day on her bed, to her arms stiffening around me.

I invented a fairy godmother who'd stay with me until I fell asleep—no magic pumpkins, no glass slippers. Just imaginary arms around me until I slept. I looked forward to bedtime. I fantasized about the prince who would come to love me, and about the fairy godmother, always there, putting me into the carriage, arranging my dress just so. I still do; I still look forward to bedtime, and I still imagine my fairy godmother taking care of me; I play a movie of her in my head.

As soon as fifth grade started, I insisted on walking to and from school by myself, even though I didn't know any other kids who got to walk alone so young. I lied to my mother and told her everyone else got to, and she believed me, even though she could easily have asked the other parents. We live so close to the school, maybe she was sure I'd be safe. Maybe she watched me from the living room window. When I look back on it, it's amazing I never walked into oncoming traffic. I'd spend those few blocks completely inside my head, imagining my fairy godmother was walking with me. And having her with me, I felt safe. She made me brave. Once, I knew I'd gone too far when, after school, I forgot she wasn't real and I poured two glasses of milk instead of just one. My mother was in the other room, hadn't seen me do it, and presumably hadn't heard me talking to the fairy godmother, but my cheeks were hot as I poured the extra milk into the sink. When I put the extra glass in the dishwasher, it felt like I was hiding something.

No one ever thought I was lying about my father—by now, half the kids in our class have divorced parents, and why would anyone invent such a mundane story? And I never leave the room or make uncomfortable faces when kids talk about their dads. Never sigh with jealousy when people complain their dads are too strict, too hard on them, too embarrassing. I laugh when people talk about the annoying things their fathers do. Everyone knows my parents had a messy divorce when I was too young to know the details, and everyone accepts that, because plenty of kids are in the same situation. But now Jeremy has broken my lie and my skin is itching, as though curiosity could be turned back on like a light.

5

It's Tuesday, and Kate's absent. Actually, she's been missing a lot of days since the school year began; I'd just never really noticed before. Now I kind of miss her. I want to spend time with the girl who thinks I'm cool, because maybe then I'll start to believe it myself.

After the physics quiz, I try to catch Jeremy's eye—I actually think I did well, and I want to thank him for his help—but it's the last class of the day, and he rushes out like he has somewhere he has to be. Probably track practice or something. Of course, Jeremy is the star of every team he joins.

At lunch on Wednesday, Jeremy sits next to me and we begin our Alexis-staring contest. I joke that we're actually losing weight too; we're so fascinated by watching her that we forget to eat.

"We've gotta get ourselves a new table," Jeremy whispers to me.

I grin, though certainly I know that if Jeremy leaves this table for another, he isn't going to take me with him. He could fit in at any table. I'm not so sure about me.

"No, seriously," he continues. "We'll start our own table. Healthy eaters only." He turns his chair around so it's facing away from the table, and I do the same. He looks around at the cafeteria.

I never counted how many tables are in here, but I can tell that Jeremy has.

"'Course, it'll be tough; most of the tables are taken."

"Yup. We'll have to get here early, claim one right away."

He winks, like we're on a mission now. "Good call."

The lunchroom is packed. There's a crowd around the table with pastries and bread on it—this means they've brought out a fresh batch of bagels that are still warm. I even see a teacher or two pushing to get to the bagel basket.

Brent Fisher is walking toward us. He's a senior, but he knows Jeremy pretty well.

"Hey, Cole, can I talk to you a second?" He crouches by Jeremy's chair.

"What's up, Fisher?"

How do boys know how to use last names like that? Makes them sound so cool.

"Well, it's about Marcy McDonald."

Marcy is a junior at another school, but everyone knows who she is. She's beautiful, and Jeremy dated her for most of sophomore year, but at the start of this year he was single. I don't think anyone knows why they broke up: the gossip mill is never as strong in the summertime; people go away—on vacation, to country houses, to fancy college-preparatory summer schools.

"I know you guys were pretty tight last year," Brent begins, and Jeremy shrugs. "But she and I were hanging out last weekend, and I . . . Well, dude, I'd really like to ask her out. But I know things ended badly between you guys—"

Hmm, I think. Really?

"—and I don't want to, you know . . ."

"Dude, don't worry about it. Marcy'd be lucky to have you."

"So we're cool?"

"Completely." Throughout this whole exchange, Brent hasn't so much as looked my way. I wonder if it's one of those unwritten laws on how to converse with royalty.

"Thanks, dude." Brent looks genuinely relieved as he turns to walk away, which makes me think that things have already moved forward with him and Marcy and he'd been scared it would get back to Jeremy before he got the okay. Huh, I think, Fornication Under Consent of the King. Just like in feudal times.

Jeremy turns back to me. "Marcy, man. Good luck with that chick."

"That must have been a bad breakup," I try, curious to know what happened, hoping he'll elaborate.

"Whatever. I'm sure she has nice qualities. I used to think so, anyway."

Maybe she cheated on him. But that's unfathomable. Why would anyone cheat on Jeremy Cole? I decide to change the subject. "Oh, I've been meaning to ask you—how's Kate doing? She's absent again today. She must not have been faking, huh? I mean, is she really sick? The flu's been going around something awful."

"Going around something awful?" Jeremy smiles wickedly. "You know, Sternin, sometimes you talk like a grandmother." I blush. "Catch you later, Granny," Jeremy says, and he gets up and heads to a different table—where he's met enthusiastically, of course. I knew he didn't mean it about starting a table of our own.

Now that the physics quiz is over and Jeremy's vocab has

improved, I wonder if maybe our—I don't know what to call it: friendship? flirtation? exchange of skills?—is over. I pretty much assume it is. It never was anything; Jeremy is just that guy who can hang out with anyone, so he just chose me for a few days there. That's all.

I am very nearly floored when the phone at home rings later and it's him. First of all, the call comes late, after eleven, and I don't really have any friends who would call that late on a school night. That's the kind of thing only your very best friend would do without worrying about getting you into trouble with your parents. I'm not particularly social once I get home at night; I'm Rapunzel, locked up in my tower to study, with no late-night callers.

I'm groggy as I say, "Hello?"

"Sternin, hey, what's up?"

"Not me." I recognize Jeremy's voice. It's thrilling to hear his voice on my phone, even if he's upset my bedtime routine.

"Huh?"

"I was half asleep, Jeremy."

"Oh, dude, it's not even midnight. Jeez, Connelly, let your hair down once in a while."

Not quite the fairy-tale request, but he is a modern-day prince after all.

"Wanna hang out?" Jeremy continues.

"Now?"

"Sure."

"It's eleven-thirty on a Wednesday night. I'm in my pajamas."

"So? I'll grab a taxi. Just stand outside with me while I have a cigarette."

Why is he compelled to take a cab all the way up here—his family lives a good thirty blocks away—to stand outside my building with me (in my pajamas) to smoke a cigarette? That'll take him less time than the trip up here. But I'm curious.

"Okay, sure."

"Great. Come down in fifteen minutes, okay?"

"Okay, see you soon."

My muscles feel so tight that I practically bounce from my bed and into the bathroom. My skin looks awful, greasy from the lotions I douse it with before I fall asleep—all kinds of clear-pore stuff that promises to prevent breakouts. My hair is dirty and flat. I should put on some makeup. I should change my clothes.

I open the front door quietly, leave it unlocked for myself, press for the elevator. I think about the kind of guy who goes out, jets uptown just for a cigarette with some girl. It's not because he's scared of getting caught smoking in his neighborhood; just as many people know him around here—maybe even more, since I live closer to school. For the Coles, a cab ride uptown just for the hell of it isn't a waste of money. They're old New York money. I heard that there's a centuries-old mansion from his mother's side of the family somewhere in New England. But maybe that's just a rumor; that's the Jewish side of the family, and I also heard that they'd immigrated here in the 1900s and made their fortune in New York real estate. The Coles know everyone and everything. I'm certain Jeremy knows how my father died. And of all the things that Jeremy has and all the things he gets to do, that's the thing I envy most.

He's in my lobby when the elevator door opens, which surprises me—cool people aren't usually so prompt.

He doesn't look like he usually does. He's wearing flannel pajama pants and they don't fit at all, unlike the rest of his perfect wardrobe. He looks scared.

"Sternin!" he calls out as I exit the elevator, though I can tell his heart's not in it. He doesn't sound happy. He turns and I follow him out the door, and he lights a cigarette expertly. I've never had a cigarette, but I don't want to admit that to him.

"Want one?" he offers.

"Sure."

He hands a cigarette to me and I put it in my mouth. He holds his lighter to the tip and I wait for the cigarette to light up. Nothing happens and I stick the tip farther into the flame.

"You gotta suck in, Sternin."

My cheeks get hot and I suck hard, but manage not to cough as I inhale. The cigarette lights and I'm relieved. Jeremy doesn't notice, or at least doesn't care, that when I inhale I blow the smoke right back out instead of breathing it all the way into my lungs.

He doesn't say anything. I'm scared that if I ask him what he's doing here, he won't come back.

He lights a second cigarette with the smoldering tip of the first before tossing the butt on the ground, something I've never seen anyone do before.

"It's nice out, huh, Sternin?"

I nod, even though I'm freezing. My cigarette's gone, so I bury my hands in my pockets. Maybe if I just wait, maybe if I'm just quiet, he'll explain why he's here.

"Sometimes I can't believe we're juniors. I still feel like I'm younger, you know?" I nod, but Jeremy's not even looking at me.

"I mean, I'm sixteen. That makes Kate twelve. Twelve! I remember when she was born."

I don't know what that's like. I don't have any siblings. I can't think of anyone I've known since she was born.

Jeremy drops his cigarette and expertly crushes it under his heel.

"Hey, Sternin, thanks for coming out tonight," he says with finality, and I think, That's it? Wait, please wait, and tell me why you asked me to come have a cigarette with you. I should say something.

"Jeremy?"

"Yeah, Connie?"

I'm kind of startled when he calls me Connie. Normally I hate being called that, and now I'm surprised to discover that I like the way it sounds when Jeremy says it. So I just say, "Have a good night."

He kisses me goodbye on the cheek, like I'm a friend of the family. He smells like smoke, and I'm kind of relieved when he disappears into a cab. This was a strange seven minutes. I felt like he was waiting for me to do something. Maybe he was waiting for me to kiss him. I've never had a guy wait for me to do that, and maybe that's how they wait. Or maybe he was waiting for me to ask him something; maybe he knows I don't know how my father died. Maybe he wants to tell me. But how would he know that I don't? And even though asking him might soothe my skin—I've even tried using extra moisturizer since this itching started—it would be beyond embarrassing. For the Coles and everyone else to know that I don't know, that I never found out, that I've been lying.

6

There are things that even the Coles don't know. Maybe they know that my dad's parents live across the country, and even that I see them for one week every August. But they don't know that when I visit them, I feel like I've been transported back to the 1950s. My grandparents still have a black-and-white TV with an antenna, and my grandmother cooks spaghetti and meatballs, and they call dinner "supper." There's white bread and margarine in the middle of the table, and Oreos and milk for dessert. And no one knows that when I was little, I would pass the time by pretending I was someplace else, usually someplace exotic; that I was a princess trapped in a mystical tower, waiting for a prince to break through the enchantment to set me free.

Every corner of my dad's parents' house reminds me of a different fantasy I had there when I was small, a different story I made up to keep myself busy. Sometimes I get caught up in the stories all over again. There are childhood pictures of my father on the living room wall, right next to my baby pictures, but they don't seem connected to my fuzzy idea of a father. I have no memory of my grandparents with him, no memory of them before my father died. They could just be a nice old couple I spend time with.

You know, if my mother could've gotten away with it, I bet I wouldn't even know that he died—like, if a girl could grow up fatherless without some kind of explanation, she wouldn't have even told me. But it's not the kind of thing you can say absolutely nothing about; only nearly nothing.

My whole body has gone curious, not just my skin. I tap my fingers on my desk while I wonder if my father's death was sudden, when I should be studying for a history exam. I chew my lip till it cracks in study hall while I wonder if he was ill and had time to put his affairs in order, or if it was sudden and my mom was left scrambling. Curiouser and curiouser: now that the switch has been flipped, it's all I can think about. I think about it until my head hurts. Sixteen seems far too old to be this clueless. Now, I'm almost ashamed that I haven't looked for answers before; now, I can't imagine going much longer without answers, can't possibly go on living with this curiosity that makes me scratch till my skin is raw and my whole body tense.

❋ ❋ ❋

Jeremy comes over on Thursday night too. By Friday night I expect his call; I'm wide awake, and I've waited to wash my face and things so that my face isn't covered in lotion. It's always the same: he smokes his cigarettes, I fake-smoke one or two, and I wait for him to explain what he's doing with me, to explain why he needs to leave his house every night. But we barely speak. I'm beginning to suspect that Kate is really sick, since she still isn't back in school, but I don't ask him about it. Now that I think it might be something serious, it would be nosy to ask; before, it seemed like just making conversation.

On Saturday, Gram—my mother's mother—takes me out to lunch. Gram always says that I don't eat enough, though she also always says to be careful to hold my stomach in when I stand up because it's sticking out. When she says things like that, I remind myself that she's had a hard life: her family died in the Holocaust after she had escaped to America, and her marriage to my grandfather was arranged because his family had a good business. They had a successful, if not happy, life together, I suppose. My grandfather made a good enough living to take care of my grandma, and there was even enough left for my mom and me after he was gone. My grandfather had a heart attack and passed away before I was born.

It's strange that I know how my mother's father died, I have some idea how Gram's whole family died, but I don't know how my own father died.

I sit across from Gram at the restaurant, both of us in flowered chairs with plush seats and hard, straight backs that Gram says are good for your posture. I wonder if Gram is proud of my mother, if the life my mother has is anything close to the life Gram wanted for her.

Maybe my father's not really dead. Maybe it's true that he and my mother had some terrible, awful divorce and she got full custody, and then she said he was dead so that I would never go look for him. Maybe he is a really terrible person. Maybe he did something really bad. There's a girl at school whose father convinced a judge that his ex-wife was insane and had her institutionalized so he could have full custody of his daughter. The truth came out, though, and the mother was released, and the girl never sees her dad anymore. It's comforting to think that the truth always comes out eventually. It soothes my curious muscles. But then they tense again, because I don't know how that truth came out; there was probably a lot of work involved: court cases, investigations, questions asked and answers found. I wish the truth would just come out on its own.

My grandmother clucks as I eat my soup, though she seems somewhat pacified by the fact that I'm also eating bread.

"Not so much butter, Connelly Jane."

Gram likes to call me Connelly Jane; Jane (or some Polish, Jewish version of it) was her sister's name.

"Gram, the butter's the best part." She smiles, because she agrees with me, and if her stomach wasn't so sensitive, she'd eat butter too.

"So, darling, I can't remember the last time you suggested we have a meal."

"Don't be silly, Gram, I see you almost every week."

"With your mother. Honestly, I think she brings you along to distract me while she goes through my china cabinet."

"You know all she wants are Grandpa's candlesticks."

"Feh. I've never kept them from her."

I don't understand; is she irritated that my mother wants the candlesticks or irritated that she hasn't taken them yet? My mother takes only the things that my grandmother suggests she take, the things Gram practically forces into our arms when we leave the apartment. Things I know my mother doesn't want, things that add clutter to our home, clutter that she hates: a china candy dish; a set of linen napkins, some of which are stained; leftover chicken soup. The candlesticks are never offered, and they're the only thing my mother wants; she's told me so. They are tall and silver, elaborate, even maybe a little gaudy. Not my mother's taste, and not mine, but they were important to her father, so now they're important to her.

"It must have been hard for her when Grandpa died, and they remind her of him."

"Why? He stopped using them a long time ago. They just sat in the cabinet. I'm the one who took them out and polished them."

"Maybe just because they were his. Because he used them when she was growing up. Maybe that's enough to remind her. I mean"—and I pause—"it's not like I remember seeing my father open a wine bottle, but the wine rack still reminds me of him."

I've made that up. It's pathetic that bottles of wine are the best I can do. But my mother never touches them—she doesn't even drink—so I can guess that the extensive, untouched, dust-covered collection by the kitchen must have belonged to him.

"Not the same thing."

"Why?" My soup has gotten cold and I only had a few spoon-fuls of it. It's not fair; my mother had the chance to build up mem-ories with her father. She doesn't need to choose the candlesticks just because they happened to be his, like me and the wine bottles.

Although, no matter what they say about "it's better to have loved and lost," maybe it's harder to lose a father you knew and loved.

Gram takes a slow sip of tea, like she's deciding what to say to me. "She only wants them because they're fancy," she says finally, trying to make it into nothing, no big deal, a joke. I want her to know I understand she's trying to lighten the mood, so I grin.

But I'm not done searching for answers, or at least clues, so I say, "Still, they mean something to her, for whatever reason. A person should have the things that remind her of her father." Gram shrugs; it's clear she doesn't see that this has anything to do with me, with my father. Maybe I lost my father so young that she doesn't consider me as even ever having had a father.

"I don't have anything that reminds me of mine," I say. Gram looks at me sharply. Under the table, I tap my left foot rapidly against my chair.

"What do you need to remember him?" she adds, then pauses, seeming startled by what she has just said. She adds quietly, "What do we need to remember anyone?"

I can hardly play the pity card with someone whose whole family is gone, even if she is my grandmother and is therefore slightly more inclined to feel sorry for me. She never had anything to remember her family by, and moreover, she doesn't need anything. I've played this all wrong. I'll never get anything out of her that she doesn't want to give me. My grandmother May love gossip, but gossips only give out information when it's fun for them.

I decide to walk home, across Central Park, where the leaves are changing and beginning to fall off the trees. I'm hoping the walk will wear me out a little, calm my body down. It's surprisingly hot, and I wish I wasn't dressed in such warm clothes. I'm thinking so hard that I get turned around and end up on Central Park South instead of Fifth Avenue. This adds about twenty minutes to the walk, but I don't care, even though I've begun to sweat. It gives me more time to think. I feel like Gram did give something away that I never saw before. Some look in her eye said something, and my feet have begun to hurt when I understand completely. When she said, "What do you need to remember him?" she didn't mean, "What do you need to remember him by?" What she meant was, "What do you need to remember him *for*?"

She doesn't think he's worth remembering. Suddenly my theory that his death is a hoax to keep him away from me seems less ridiculous. I mean, I don't think that's it—I believe that he's dead—but there's something he did that she's angry about, something she's ashamed of. Some reason he's not worth remembering.

7

Jeremy doesn't come over for his nightly cigarette, but that doesn't surprise me, since it's Saturday. Surely he has better things to do on a Saturday night: hot parties, hot girls. Princes don't get carded, so I'm sure he's at one of those fabulous Manhattan spots, dancing with the latest It Girl, or at least with members of her entourage.

And the thing is, I'm not jealous, not exactly. I have a lot of work to do—I may have the verbal half of the SATs down, but the math is still kicking my ass. But I do wonder what that sort of life would be like. I don't want to live that way all the time, but maybe once in a while—be bad, freak my mother out by coming home at four in the morning, try drinking or smoking pot and just seeing what it is about being one of the cool kids that's so appealing.

Jeremy would never invite me—I'm the girl he smokes private cigarettes with, sits with for a few minutes during lunch. I'm not a girl he'd invite to go partying. Even if he wanted to, he wouldn't, because I'm sure I don't seem the type who would go. It'd be too embarrassing for him, for me, for everyone.

On Sunday, my mother and I have brunch. As we walk to the restaurant, I wonder what would happen if I asked her about my father, if I asked her how he died. But after so many years of silence on the topic, I'm not about to just bring it up over bagels and lox. But I wonder what would happen if I did.

We order, and she waits until the food comes to broach the subject I'm sure she'd been dying to talk about for a while now.

"So, is Jeremy Cole going to be coming over to study this week?"

I think it's funny that she calls him by his full name. I decide to do the same. "I doubt it. Jeremy Cole was helping me with physics, and I think he's gotten my grade up."

"That certainly was nice of him."

"Yeah, well, I was helping him with the SATs."

My mother laughs. "Oh, honey, I'm sure you were, but you know the Coles can afford a private tutor." She's not saying this to be mean—she means it like, See, that was just his excuse to get to spend time with you, because he likes you.

I try to pretend that I haven't been thinking the same thing myself. I try to pretend that I'm not every bit as curious as she is about his sudden interest in me.

"I know they can, but I think he was just trying to make me feel better about needing help in physics."

"What a gentleman." She takes a bite of her food. "Of course, it's such a shame about the daughter."

I look up at her sharply. "The daughter? Do you mean Kate?"

"Yes. Oh, honey, haven't you heard?" I shake my head. "Well, I don't know the details of it, but apparently she's very sick. Didn't you know? Hasn't she been missing school lately?"

"Yeah." I chew thoughtfully. "I haven't seen her, actually, in almost a week. More."

"Oh dear. They're such a lovely family." I nod, not really paying attention anymore (honestly, what does it matter whether they're a lovely family or not?), but wondering what's the matter with Kate, what kind of sickness she has. Kate, the girl who thinks I'm cool. And pretty.

My mother continues, "You know my friend Marian?" I nod. "Well, she's friends with Ellie Swift, who's practically best friends with Joanie Cole, Jeremy's mom?" I nod again. "Well, apparently Ellie told Marian that Kate Cole is sick—she wouldn't tell her with what, didn't want to betray Joanie's confidence."

"It's a little late for that," I cut in, realizing as I say it how mean it sounds.

My mother looks startled. "What? Well anyhow, it's quite serious. Marian said obviously Joanie's in denial about it, but she—Marian—can tell it's really very serious."

My mother could be a seventh grader, sharing gossip by the lockers. In my head, I see her in a pleated skirt, textbooks in her arms; I picture her gossiping with Marian and Ellie outside the lunchroom. I try not to wonder about Kate. With my mother's tendency toward hyperbole, Kate's illness might be something relatively minor, like a severe case of the flu or something—enough to keep her out of school, but nothing that could do any permanent damage. Jeremy would have told me if there was anything more serious.

Well, actually, of course he wouldn't. He never tells me anything about himself, and come to think of it, I never tell him anything about myself. We limit our conversations to school, studying, and Anorexic Alexis. That's pretty much it.

And certainly if it was serious, Jeremy wouldn't have come by to smoke every night like that. He would have been home with his family. Why would he want to stand on a corner with me at a time like that?

My mother and I go shopping after brunch. We walk down Madison, from the Eighties to the Seventies, stopping in little boutiques along the way. My mother is on an accessories kick. She picks out belts, and for the first time I notice that maybe her fashion sense isn't as perfect as I used to think. She always seemed so glamorous to me: the best-dressed mom when she took me to school, not like the moms who showed up in the morning wearing sweats or leggings, looking like they just got out of bed. No, my mother had outfits; she dressed up for everything. Now I wonder who she was trying to impress. She picks out shoes much flashier than I would ever wear, and I'm a teenager. I want to tell her they're not right, but I think she'd get mad, or hurt. So I keep my thoughts to myself and we continue down Madison, on to the next store. In the Seventies, there's one block where the sidewalk is paved differently than it is anyplace else. The cement literally shines in the sunlight; there are sparkles on the sidewalk. When I was little, I used to imagine the street was paved with gold and silver for the princes and princesses walking across it, and even for me. I concentrate on it now, squinting at the sparkles, still not quite understanding how or why they paved it that way.

❈ ❈ ❈

Later, while my mom is still shopping, I decide to do some amateur detective work at home. Like, really amateur—my detective work is limited to going through the drawers in my mother's desk, a piece of furniture I'd never really taken notice of before; it always seemed more decorative than functional. My mother takes up most of the apartment—on phone calls, she literally paces from one end to the other, snaking her way in and out of each room, even the bathrooms. Her clothes take up the closets in her bedroom, the ones by the front door, and even part of the closets in my room. I don't think she could possibly confine anything of importance to something as small as this desk.

But still, its three drawers are the only place I can think to start looking, even if I've never actually seen her sit there.

The first drawer is full of envelopes and stamps—old stamps, like twenty-five-cent ones that would barely get a postcard to its destination now. And old greeting cards: not cards she's received, but cards I'm sure she intended to send to people—blank birthday cards and anniversary cards and get-well-soon cards. I'm sure my mother bought them all so that she'd have a supply on hand when the need arose, but I'm equally certain she has no memory that they're here. Or maybe she's just stocked up this drawer because she believes that a woman should have such a supply at her disposal.

The second drawer, I'm surprised to find, has old pictures of mine—not photographs of me, but drawings with crayon and marker that I made when I was much younger. I find my kindergarten diploma, which isn't really a diploma so much as a piece of construction paper on which we'd drawn pictures of ourselves and over which our teacher wrote "Kindergarten Diploma." When I was little, my now-dark hair had flecks of blond in it, and I notice that I'd tried to show this in my picture by using both brown and yellow markers for my hair. The result makes it look like I had a group of bumblebees attacking my skull. I take it from the drawer to save it. I'm sure that my mother won't miss it.

The third drawer is photographs. My mother has albums, but she never fills them properly, and ends up leaving photos around the apartment: stuck between books on shelves, piled up in a basket in the kitchen and on top of her bedstand, crammed into her jewelry box. She may hate clutter, but she's still not particularly organized. The photos in the desk are older, like maybe she stuffed them in here when she cleared up the piles of photos that she'd left around the house we lived in before my father died, before we moved into Gram's apartment. There are baby pictures of me, pictures of her from when she was in college, pictures of her when she was pregnant and of my grandparents holding me not long after I was born. And there are pictures of my father, of course. There's one of him holding me as a baby; one with both my parents in which it looks like they were off to a costume party—he's dressed as a football player, she as a cheerleader. And there is one of the two of them sitting in a chair, my mother on my father's lap. It must have been taken in the seventies or early eighties: their outfits make me laugh. Both of their pants flare out at the bottom. My mother is smiling at the camera and my father is smiling in another direction, like he's in conversation with someone across the room, his arms twist around her back. I don't know why, but this picture means more to me than the ones I find from their wedding day, of the three of us together, of my father holding me while I sleep. I don't take any of them except for this one of the two of them. I think I like it best because they just look like any other young couple. There's no gravity to it, no wedding ceremony or new baby, and certainly no awareness that their time together would be limited. They were just a pair of young people spending time with friends. It's comforting to think of them this way—there's nothing special about them; they weren't marked, somehow; you couldn't tell that they were going to come to a sad end. Maybe they weren't even married or engaged yet in this picture. They were just hanging out, the way I would like to someday with a boyfriend.

I tuck the picture into my copy of *A Farewell to Arms,* next to a paragraph about having enough love so that you never have to feel lonely. I wonder if my mother is lonely. She wasn't my mother yet in this picture; she wasn't much older than I am now—maybe my age exactly. Maybe my parents were high school sweethearts. I know that they grew up together, lived only a few blocks away from each other here in the city. My mother went to an all-girls school, though, so they can't have gone to school together. It occurs to me that he might have been the only man she ever loved. If he'd lived, who knows what might have happened between them—maybe they'd have had more kids, or maybe they'd have fought, had affairs, gotten bored with each other and divorced. But no doubt my mother believes that she would have lived a happy life with him, had he lived. It must be incredibly lonely, believing that.

I know that I haven't found anything to help me on my search, nothing other than some evidence that my parents were in love. And that is something, but it has nothing to do with how he died, and that's supposed to be what I'm looking for. I didn't think I would find anything, but I'm disappointed anyway, because I'm not at all sure where to go next.

Luckily, Jeremy calls that night from a taxi to tell me that he's on the way over for a cigarette, which provides a nice distraction.

I should, I know, be angry with Jeremy, or at least irritated at his audacity—calling me every night of the week except Saturday, when he had something better to do. And angry at myself for always being here, always being available. The truth is, I never have anything better to do than to stand outside my lobby while he smokes. Even when I go to a movie or something with girls from school, I'm home by around ten. And somehow Jeremy knew that about me—not only does he know it now that we've been hanging out, but even before, it never occurred to him that I might have had a reason to say no to him. I guess princes don't ever expect to hear the word "no."

As I step out of the elevator, cross the lobby, and get hit with a chilly burst of evening air coupled with the odor of cigarette smoke, I decide that I should, in fact, be very, very angry at Jeremy and that it is not okay to treat me like this, to invite himself over. Tonight he has called me from the cab on his way here—he didn't even call first to make sure I was available, to make sure I wanted to see him.

I should be angry. A popular girl, a confident girl, would be angry—not excited to see him again, not excited that this isn't finished, even though he didn't come over last night.

He's crushing a cigarette under his heel. When he sees me, he lights two cigarettes, holds one out to me. I take it but don't put it in my mouth, and I try to ignore what has struck me as a very intimate gesture—his lighting my cigarette in his mouth. Even if I'm not really mad, I can try to pretend.

"Jeremy, you know, what if I was busy, or sleeping or something?"

"Then I would have told the cabdriver to turn around."

"Dude, that's just not okay. I'm not one of those girls. . . . I'm not Marcy McFuckingDonald, okay? I'm not your girlfriend and I'm not just here at your disposal every evening for a cigarette break. I have a life, you know."

Jeremy doesn't seem even ruffled. "What did I interrupt, then?" he asks, and he makes it sound polite.

I look at the ground, embarrassed. "That's not the point."

I look up and Jeremy smiles crookedly, just one side of his mouth up. "I know, Sternin. But shouldn't it be?"

It's really hard not to smile back at him. I can feel the sides of my lips curling up, both of them. I can't even manage just a half smile, like he did.

"It's just not nice, Jeremy. It's not nice to just come over, to expect that I'll be available like this." I stop myself before I say that I don't even know him, that we're not even friends. Bad enough that I said that I wasn't his girlfriend, cementing the fact.

"Do you want me to stop coming over?" He says it politely, softly. Not like a threat. He says it like he means it, even though he must know, as well as I do, that I would never say yes.

"That's not what I meant."

He smokes silently for a few minutes. I drop my cigarette to the ground, unsmoked except for Jeremy's having lit it.

"I know you're not Marcy McDonald. If you were anything like Marcy McDonald, I wouldn't be here."

"God, what did she do to you?" I'm surprised at myself for asking flat out, just like that, but something about Jeremy made me feel entitled to ask. Like, You come to my house every night, I let you intrude on my life, you know how my fucking father died, don't you, so at least tell me what Marcy did. It's not like I'm asking whether the rumors about Kate being sick are true. If they even qualify as rumors. It's just something my mother said.

Jeremy doesn't say anything.

"Come on, dude, it's not like she cheated on you."

Jeremy looks straight at me, exhaling smoke. "How do you know that?"

"Who would she cheat with? Brad bloody Pitt?" I'm embarrassed that I'm flattering him. And I'm embarrassed by my use of the word "bloody." I expect Jeremy to make fun of me for it. I don't know where it came from; it sounds like something one of the characters in my fantasies might have said. Sometimes I make my fairy godmother British.

But Jeremy just smiles and says, "Nah, too old. He's so nineties."

"Well, I don't know, then—whoever. She wouldn't cheat on you. No girl is that stupid." What am I saying? I sound pathetic; I sound like I feel privileged just to get to see him so close-up. "I just mean, you know everyone. It would totally get back to you. And you could totally decimate her reputation, and that's important to a girl like that. I mean, it's even important to me."

"So I shouldn't decimate your reputation?" He's teasing me.

This conversation is so frustrating that my lips are raw, since I bite my lower lip every time Jeremy speaks. I was supposed to be angry at him for showing up rudely; I was supposed to be acting more confident.

And really, why am I being so nosy about his breakup with Marcy? I like gossip just fine, but I'm not like my mother or Gram: I don't seek it out; I don't really relish it. The fact is, this is none of my business. But I feel entitled to know about it, like how people in kingdoms feel entitled to know what's going on in the lives of their royals. Like all the tabloids in Britain sharing the secrets of the Windsors. People probably couldn't explain why they care, but they still think they have a right to know.

Finally Jeremy says something seriously. "Connie, it was nothing. I just thought I could trust her, and it turned out I couldn't."

"So that means she cheated, right?"

Jeremy shakes his head. "No, kid, it doesn't mean she cheated."

"You can be a real pain in the ass, Jeremy. I'm trying to have a conversation here. You don't have to act like I'm your little sister."

He grins slyly. "My little sister knows why we broke up."

And he leans down and kisses me on the cheek, but he holds his lips there a second longer than is casual, leans in a little more. His hand squeezes my upper arm, and the pressure of it is comforting. It feels, actually, like the kind of squeeze you might give your little sister, and funnily enough, I kind of wish I could be. How nice to have a boy like this looking out for you, teaching you who you have to steer clear of; telling you about high school parties and what goes on there, that maybe it's okay to drink and do some drugs—

just make sure it doesn't get out of hand, and of course you can sit in the lounge with the upperclassmen, no one will cross me.

Well, I guess I'm a cliché, a fatherless girl longing to be taken care of by the boy she finds attractive. Nah, for it to be a real cliché, he'd have to be much older.

"See you tomorrow, Con," Jeremy says, releasing my arm and walking to the corner. I watch him stick his hand out for a cab and I wait until he climbs into one before I turn to walk into my building. Like I need some assurance that he's going to get home safely or something.

8

It's raining on Monday. I guess we've been lucky so far that when Jeremy's come for a cigarette, it hasn't rained. I guess it was only a matter of time. Jeremy sits with me at lunch. Alexis isn't even there today, so there's no excuse for the way that we sit without talking.

But everyone around us is talking.

"I swear to God, she's in the hospital."

"No way."

"They said it was anorexia—"

"Who said?"

"How the hell should I know? But anyway, I heard it was really coke."

"Heard from where?" Jeremy cuts in. Jeremy and I think we know better. We've been watching her. We know it's anorexia.

It was Brent Fisher who said that, and he's obviously embarrassed. Emily Winters comes to his rescue. "It's true. I heard Mrs. Downing on the phone with her mother." This has to be a lie. Why would Alexis's parents tell the faculty it was coke? If anyone had heard anything, it would have been from one of Alexis's friends. Emily tries to loop me in. "I meant to tell you about it, Connelly, this morning."

I shrug. "I haven't heard anything." Emily looks disappointed in me, and I feel bad that I didn't take her side. Jeremy touches my shoulder before he gets up to leave.

❀ ❀ ❀

Kate isn't in school either, but no one's whispering about her, at least not out in the open. I guess a sick seventh grader isn't exactly fodder for the rumor mill like an anorexic coke addict.

In physics, the formulas swim over my head and it's all I can do not to beg Jeremy to tutor me again. The chairs in the physics lab aren't really chairs but stools, with desks so high they come up to my chest when I'm standing. I swing my legs from the high stool, which makes me feel even younger, even more clueless, like I'm way too little to be in this grown-up class where everything is so hard. After class, I look to Jeremy for help, for some reassuring look that he understands everything and he's here to help, but he's surrounded by two guys and Nina Zuckerman, the most beautiful girl in our class, and maybe the most beautiful girl I've ever seen in real life. She's wearing almost the same thing I'm wearing—jeans and a tank top under a cardigan sweater—but the outfit looks so different on her, so thoughtlessly stylish that you can tell it takes effort for me to dress right but she doesn't even have to try. I couldn't possibly go up to him in those circumstances. I can only take his help if he offers it.

❀ ❀ ❀

I'm spending a free period in the library, and it occurs to me that there must be records somewhere about my father's death. The school has a bunch of old newspapers on microfiche; maybe I can just find his obituary. It's such a simple idea that I feel stupid not to have thought of it before. The microfiche are still organized by card catalog, unlike the rest of the library. I guess no one ever has cause to look at the *New York Times* from over a decade ago. I'm about to open the card catalog when I realize that I don't know the exact date of my father's death. He died after I turned two; that's all I know. I wish I could remember the funeral, at least—if I could remember what I wore (if I went), maybe that would help me figure out what time of year it was. I've never been taught how to use a card catalog—everything's computerized now—and I'm embarrassed to ask the librarian for help. She's practically senile anyway, with glasses thick like Coke bottles, her gray hair cropped close to her head. I can't imagine she would have the wherewithal to help me. And I can't imagine admitting to that woman, the one with the bad glasses and the unflattering haircut, why I need help, that I'm looking for my father's obituary. If she asked why, I could just pass it off as senti-mentality, not give away that I don't know how he died. But I'm sure she'd see through me, that she'd know I was searching for some-thing I'm not supposed to know. She'd hesitate. She probably doesn't even know that my father's dead. She'd react with shocked sympa-thy, put her doughy arm around me. I would be mortified when she refused to help me. Maybe she'd suggest that I ask my mother.

I've been standing in front of the card catalog for more than five minutes now. My hands hang at my sides—I haven't even pretended to know where to begin, which drawer to reach for. I think I might cry. And I am completely startled to feel a hand on my shoulder. Of course it's Jeremy. Of course I make an awkward inhaling/grunting noise as I turn to face him, stifling the lump in my throat. I try to play it off.

"You scared me."

"How?"

"Because I didn't know anyone was there."

"Yeah, you looked like you were concentrating pretty hard."

Sometimes I can't tell whether he's teasing me or being serious.

"Listen, Con, I thought I might come over tonight—say around eleven, for a cigarette?" He grins. "See, I'm giving you advance notice. I bet you thought I wasn't listening."

The way he's made this so simple makes me feel foolish for ever having thought it mattered. His hand has slid from my shoulder to my upper arm, and his grip feels warm. It's something out of a fairy tale: the prince deigns to touch the lowly commoner, making her weak in the knees. I have to extricate myself from his hold before he notices.

"Well, okay. See you later." I step back, freeing my arm, and bump into the card catalog. One of the drawers slides open. It smells like it hasn't been opened in years. Now my elbow hurts and my face is hot with embarrassment. Jeremy, the consummate gentleman, pretends not to notice.

"Hey, don't take it the wrong way, but I couldn't help noticing you looked kinda lost in physics. Want to study sometime this week, maybe during lunch?"

I'm grateful for the offer, though it occurs to me that it's just because of lunch today—without Alexis there to stare at, there was no excuse for our sitting next to each other in silence. Studying would cover up the awkwardness.

"Yes, okay, perfect."

"Okay, see you tonight."

I wait until he walks away to rub my elbow.

It's still raining when I walk home from school and still raining when my phone rings at a quarter to eleven. I figure Jeremy's used to seeing me in my pajamas by now, so I don't even bother with shoes; I shuffle downstairs in my slippers. Jeremy and I huddle under the awning of the building, just outside the lobby.

"It's freezing," he says.

"Yeah, what are we going to do in a few weeks? It'll be November." I immediately regret having said this, having admitted to some assumption that this will keep going on. Jeremy doesn't seem to notice the weight of what I said. He jokes, "We'll just have to huddle closer."

I know it's a joke, but it's one that, being a girl who has admitted attraction to the boy standing a few feet away from her, I read a lot into. Like, does that mean he thinks that by November we'll be more likely to be standing close, i.e., hooking up or dating or at least being comfortable buddies who don't mind getting close to keep warm? Because whether we're buddies now or not, there's nothing comfortable going on here. I can't imagine even taking one step closer to him. The most intimate thing he's ever done is light a cigarette for me in his mouth together with his own.

God, how come he knows how my father died and I don't even know if it's okay to lean against him when I'm cold?

And then, just like that, he gives me something intimate: "Jesus Christ," he says, and I can see he's choked up. Visibly choked up. (Obviously, visibly—otherwise, how the hell would I know?)

And having been given this window, I have no idea what to do. And I only have a second to figure it out.

"Jeremy?" I offer dumbly. I'm so flustered; this moment has so much responsibility. A guy like Jeremy Cole is never ruffled. Hell, it's his job, as prince, to show a good outward appearance at all times. If he is showing this to me, he must either trust me or be so upset that he simply can't hold it in.

I know he'll compose himself before he reveals anything. So I just wait.

"Jesus. Christ," he says again, this time much more slowly. He's looking down at the pavement.

"I just really love her, you know?"

Jeremy is still looking down, so I stand nearer to him—he's taller than I am, so even if he is looking down, if I stand close enough, he'll be looking at me.

"Jeremy?"

"What did you do? I mean, I know it's totally different, but you're all right, you're here and you're fine, so it must be okay, somehow. There must be a way to make it okay."

I am so confused that it's making me nervous. My hands are sweaty, even though I'd been so cold before.

"Jeremy, I'm sorry, but I don't understand."

"When your dad was sick—I know you were young, but you must remember. What was it like?"

What was it like. When my dad was sick. I have no clue. But I can't let Jeremy see that I don't know. I will have to think about that later. So I just say, "I'm sorry, Jeremy, I was two years old."

Jeremy looks straight at me.

"But you're okay now."

He seems to need me to affirm this, so I say, "Yes. I'm okay now."

I should say something more; something comforting. But I can't think of anything else. I must have said something right, because he nods, and then he smiles at me. He reaches his arm toward me, and for a second I think he's going to take my hand. But instead he takes the cigarette from my fingers, which seems even more intimate. It's gone out—I hadn't even noticed. Rain must have fallen on it.

"I better go," he says, crushing the cigarette in his fingers. "It's getting late, and you've got school tomorrow." He grins.

"Yes, sir, and I have to get my beauty rest." Like I'm royalty too.

I shuffle away in my slippers, go back to bed to stare at the ceiling. My father was sick. My father had an illness. Why is my mother so scared to tell me that? It's so normal. It's so banal. I think I might be disappointed.

I am nearly asleep when I realize what I missed: Jeremy was talking about Kate.

9

In the morning, every decision seems fraught. Cereal for breakfast? Moisturizing shampoo or deep-cleansing? Should I put on makeup? What should I wear? Because whatever else I do, I must wear the right thing today. I'm convinced that the right outfit will show Jeremy I'm sympathetic, but the wrong one will somehow have the power to tell the entire student body that something is wrong with Kate.

Because I'm fairly convinced that this is something of a secret. Maybe the family is trying to keep it secret; maybe he hasn't told anyone, and maybe he's trusting me. Maybe whatever Kate has is whatever my father had, and maybe her family is just as ashamed as mine.

I try to think of illnesses that people associate with shame. All that occurs to me is AIDS, and that was only in the 1980s, before people knew what they know now. I mean, sure there are people who would still think it's shameful, but not the Coles. They're a liberal New York family. They hold fund-raisers for Democratic candidates in their apartment. I remember that in one of my favorite childhood books, there was a girl with diabetes and she kept it secret because she was scared of what her friends would think.

But of course, the lesson was always that no one would care; they loved her anyway. And everyone would rally around Kate. She's every bit as beloved a princess as Jeremy is a prince.

I ransack my closet and I wonder why Jeremy said what he did exactly—that I got through it, that my father died but I'm okay now. Whatever Kate has, even if it's what my father had, surely there's some treatment now, some way to make it something she can, at least, live with. Whatever it is, it won't kill Kate—the Coles can afford the best doctors in the world; fly her to Switzerland for the most cutting-edge treatment; hire twenty-four-hour-a-day home care; give her anything she needs.

In the end, I wear jeans. Jeans are so innocuous, and I think it's innocuous that I'm going for. I pull them on—tight over my hips, looser around my ankles. I even choose the pair that I've decided is a particularly ordinary shade of blue, even though they're last year's jeans, and not nearly stylish enough.

If I look plain enough, then it won't look like anything out of the ordinary has happened. But then I think, as I pull my hair into a ponytail, as I deliberately avoid the mascara next to the bathroom sink, that maybe this is too plain. I don't want Jeremy to think that I don't care. I want him to know that I understand he was talking about Kate—that I understand him and I know how much this matters. So I put on some lip gloss, but only a little, because I also don't want him to think this is somehow exciting to me; that I'm curious, selfish, longing for gossip. And certainly the right outfit can't help me figure out what I'm supposed to say to him.

There is no right way to handle this situation.

❈ ❈ ❈

Physics is first period. Jeremy is never early to class like I am. They don't let us into the science classrooms until the teacher shows up, because there are Bunsen burners and all kinds of chemicals in there, and I guess they're worried about what we'll touch. So it's me and the early nerds waiting outside the room for Mr. Kreel, ready to rush in and get the good seats. I'm staring at my feet, and for the first time I think that maybe it's strange that our school is carpeted.

By the time Jeremy gets to class, I'm sitting perched in the second row, my notebook and pen at the ready, and the teacher is at the front of the room, waiting for everyone to settle down. It's only the cool kids who wait until the last minute to settle. I swing my legs back and forth on the stool, but then I realize I'm irritating everyone else in my row, so I stop. But then I start clicking my pen so the tip comes in and out, which is probably even more irritating.

Jeremy sits behind me like he always does, so I don't see his face until class is over and we're packing up. I'm in full panic mode because nothing that Mr. Kreel said today made sense to me. I want to ask Jeremy for help, but I'm also scared to talk to him, because I don't know the right things to say.

But he leaves the room without looking at me. I watch his back. How can he be so calm when I'm so nervous? I've been so worried all morning about looking, saying, and doing the right thing that I haven't even thought about my father, and that seems wrong too. I should care about what I now know: he was ill. There was no terrible fall, no fatal accident: he was sick. He was sick, and I think the only reason Jeremy sought me out in the lunchroom that day was because whatever he had is like whatever Kate has and Jeremy thought there might be some wisdom I could impart about how you get through the death of a loved one. He never thought I was cool; he never cared about helping me with physics. That doesn't make me angry; he was looking for help from me. But I was two years old; a two-year-old doesn't even know enough to know that she's getting through something. And I'm just as clueless now. At sixteen, I still haven't gotten past what happened to my father. How can I have gotten past it when I don't know what it is?

I think that whatever's wrong with Kate can somehow tell me what was wrong with my dad.

At lunch, Jeremy finds me at the usual table. I'm waiting for him; I have my physics book with me in case we start working. I hurried so I'd be here if he came looking for me. I didn't even grab food. Now that he's here, I realize I'm starving and glance hungrily at the bagel table.

"Sternin. Still no Alexis?" He sits beside me.

"Nope."

"Well, rehab, you know. She'll be back in twenty-eight days."

"That's the standard. Of course, the really sick ones stay longer."

"Of course."

Neither of us thinks this banter is particularly funny, since neither of us thinks that Alexis had a drug problem. I decide to test the waters.

"It's hard, you know, to see someone making herself sick like that when there are people we love who didn't have a choice in the matter."

I can't believe I really just said that. I certainly don't mean it. But I go on.

"Maybe," I continue, "that's why we're so fascinated by her when everyone else needs to think it was a drug problem, you know?"

Jeremy shrugs. "Listen, Sternin, no offense, but I don't like to talk about shit like this in school."

I'm embarrassed now for bringing it up, for asking that question.

"I'm sorry."

"It's okay—I probably should . . . I don't know." He looks around the cafeteria. Everyone seems to be having so much more fun than we are. Jeremy would never transform all the kids into knights and ladies, the teachers into earls and duchesses. He'd never understand if I told him that I give the different teachers' lounges names like the Earldom of Literary Greats, the Duchy of Scientific Stresses. He doesn't see a royal court; he just sees girls in their short skirts, with tall boots and just the right shoulder bags; boys in baseball caps and loose jeans. How does everyone else spend the time that I spend spinning in my head? I would be bored; then I would be lonely.

Three sophomores walk right past us, blatantly staring at Jeremy. I try not to laugh when one of them slips on her high heel. We're not supposed to wear high heels to school, and her skirt is so short I can almost see her underwear. Jeremy raises his eyebrows at me to show that he doesn't find that attractive.

"You looked freaked-out in physics today," he says finally.

I'm relieved, both for the help he's offering and because this is a topic I know how to talk about. "Oh God, I really, really was. I didn't know what was going on."

"Not to worry, though it doesn't look like we're going to get anything done during lunch. Let's get in some tutoring before tonight's cig break—I'll come over around eight, okay?"

Jeremy is a Physics Knight in Shining Armor.

"Okay."

"Later, Sternin." And Jeremy leans over and kisses me on the cheek goodbye. In front of everyone. In the lunchroom. I press my calves back against the metal legs of the chair, make myself stay seated, like that kiss was nothing at all.

After school, I change into my pajamas and swallow three Advil without water, hoping that it will cure my new headache, hoping it will go away before Jeremy gets here. I lie on top of the blankets on my bed. They never deal with emotional complexity in fairy tales. Like, how did Cinderella forgive her father—not for dying, but for not putting her first when he chose the woman he would marry? How did Snow White deal with knowing that her beauty led another woman to such madness? How did Rapunzel survive being locked in a tower, not only imprisoned but never able to set her feet on the ground, something that would drive most people crazy? Did she ever run her hands along the stone floor, wondering what dirt would feel like? Did she ever consider jumping out that window? Did she ever want to cut off her own hair, a fairy-tale version of cutting off your nose to spite your face? And, most intriguing and damaging of all, what about her relationship with that wicked witch? How do we even know she was wicked? The witch fed her and put a roof over her head, high and solitary though it might have been.

I prop myself up on my pillows, twist my neck so I can see out the window. We're twelve floors up, and my bedroom looks out onto Madison Avenue. Sometimes, from this window, I can see my mother coming home from one of her lunches, a walk, the supermarket. Sometimes we go to the market together, but whenever I'm not with her, she still picks up exactly the foods I want; I never have to tell her. She knew when I switched from regular Coke to Diet Coke, and started buying it for me. She notices when we're running low on cereal, even though she doesn't eat it, and always makes sure there's a fresh box and non-expired milk. Maybe the witch thought she was protecting Rapunzel, not punishing her. Maybe she thought that if Rapunzel was locked away, no one could ever hurt her. Maybe the witch kept Rapunzel because she loved her, because she was scared that if other people could get to Rapunzel, they would hurt her. And maybe Rapunzel didn't understand the witch; maybe she was angry at her—but maybe she loved her too.

10

Jeremy rings the doorbell at eight exactly. He's in general much more prompt than I would expect him to be.

"Hey, the doorman didn't buzz you."

"Nah, they know me by now."

"Yeah, I guess." Of course, all those cigarettes.

Jeremy whips out his physics textbook as soon as he gets to my room, so there's no question of talking first. I'm relieved—I'd actually done the same thing: I'd laid out all my physics stuff so that it would be waiting when he got here. I'm still embarrassed by what happened at lunch, when I tried to talk about Kate and my father.

"Where's your mom?" he asks after an hour or so of working. We're sitting on the floor by my bed, and Jeremy's leaning back against it.

I shrug. "Not sure. She wasn't home when I got home from school."

"Don't you wonder?"

"Not really. I mean, it's her private life, right? She's entitled to it."

Jeremy looks at me strangely. "You mean, she's on a date?"

"I don't know. She could be."

"But you wouldn't ask?"

I would never ask. I shrug to play it off like it's nothing. "I guess not."

"Maybe she doesn't want you to know if she's dating someone. I mean, like, she's worried you'll feel bad about it."

"I don't think I would. She's never dated anyone seriously that I know of."

Jeremy tilts his neck so the back of his head rests on top of my bed, stares at my ceiling. I think of all the times I've spent lying there, looking at the ceiling above my bed, and I wonder if Jeremy's noticing the things I see—the places where the paint is peeling, the watermark shaped like a dog's tail.

"But don't you know how strange that sounds—that you 'know of'? She's your mother."

This is getting frustrating, someone attacking our carefully choreographed cohabitation. I know some mothers and daughters are closer. And yes, it makes me jealous, even at my age, when I see them out together, holding hands. But I know that we can't be like that, not since I was a baby, not since the first day of third grade. Maybe there are too many secrets between us: she can't tell me the truth about my father; I can't tell her how I've been lying about him—about her too, and about me—since I was eight years old.

I try to act nonchalant, but I can feel my muscles tense as I answer him. "I don't know, I guess we're not close. We respect each other's privacy. She doesn't ask what I'm doing, leaving every night at eleven."

"Well, that's weird too."

"Well, we're a weird pair, what can I tell you? Whatever we're doing, it works for us." I'm exasperated now. "See how normal you'd be if your dad-slash-husband died." I'm immediately sorry for saying this, because Kate is sick, and for all I know Jeremy might have to find out what his family will be like after a death in it.

"I'm sorry, Jeremy, I didn't mean to be——" I search for the word. I can't think of one to use that won't reference Kate's illness.

"No, it's okay. I was being rude. It's none of my business how your family copes with its loss."

"I know we're strange." I'm so close to telling him that I don't know about my dad, but the embarrassment takes over. "Most families aren't like ours."

"Not like mine either."

I smile, thinking of their millions of dollars, of their power and prestige. Royal families are a rarity; of course there aren't many like his.

Jeremy sits up, presses the heel of his hand to his forehead.

"I mean, my mother can barely acknowledge what's happening. She just keeps shopping and going to her lunches and to her charity board meetings and whatever. Even when Kate's in the hospital. I mean, she visits her and stays with her too; she's not a bad mom. But Kate was diagnosed months ago, and still it's like she can't stand to let this disrupt her . . . I don't know, her place in society. And my father—he's still going to his board meetings; he even went on a business trip last month. Like they don't think they should be soaking up every second they can—you know, just in case."

"Maybe your parents know something you don't," I say carefully.

"What?"

"Well, maybe the doctors have told them something you don't know yet."

Jeremy smiles, but it's a hopeless kind of smile. I guess if there was some promising news, his parents wouldn't exactly have kept it from him.

"I was the one—" He pauses, swallows hard. "No one told her, what she had, how sick she was. Like it would be easier for her that way. They finally told her what she had, but they didn't tell her everything about it. I was the only one—I had to tell her the truth. My parents kept walking around like it was an easy fix. But when she asked me, I told her the truth. It wasn't fair. I mean, there she was, Googling her disease, trying to find out what it meant. If it were me—I would have been more scared, you know, not knowing how serious it was."

"Jeremy," I say, feeling brave, "what's wrong with Kate? I mean, you never said—what is she sick with?"

Jeremy looks at the floor. "She has leukemia. Same as your dad."

Same as my dad. My dad had leukemia. I always thought of that as something kids had, but of course adults can have it too. Of course they can.

I begin to cry. There's none of the usual warning, no lump rising in my throat, no tears building up slowly. Suddenly I'm just crying harder than I can ever remember crying. I don't know if I'm crying for my dad; for my mom, out I don't know where or with whom; for Kate, the sweet princess who's sick; for Jeremy, who could lose the sister he loves; or for myself.

And if I'm crying for myself, I don't know why either. Because

I miss my dad? How can I, when I don't remember him? Am I crying because Jeremy told me what my family couldn't? Because I'm relieved that the search is finally over? *Is* my search over? Am I crying because I miss my mother, even though I see her every day?

I don't see him move, but just like that, Jeremy has slid across the hardwood floor and he's hugging me tight. He must have some built-in big-brother ability to hug so fast like that. My shoulder where his chin rests is wet, so I know he's crying too, and so I don't even try to stop. I don't try to cover up or pretend it's nothing. We're both crying hard and messily. There's snot on my face, and I'm not even embarrassed when I wipe it on his shirt because I know it's on Jeremy's face too. Who knew a prince could cry so much?

I don't know how much times passes, but eventually we both stop and we're out of breath.

"Can I ask you something?" I want his permission first.

"Sure."

"How is Kate—now, I mean?"

"She's back at home, but she's not . . . They cut her hair, Con. She loved her hair, but they cut it so that it won't be so messy when it starts falling out. She cried the whole time. I held her hand and she cried. My mother hired some famous hairdresser to do it, and Kate made a joke that it was a waste of a good cut when it was only temporary"—he smiles, remembering her joke—"and I said nothing was ever wasted on her. It was just so hard, you know, 'cause I had to pretend like it wasn't a big deal when I was just as upset about it as she was."

I think about that hair—long, blond, wavy; the kind of hair every girl wishes she had.

"It must have been awful."

"I'm stupid enough to think that it must be harder for me and my parents than it is for her. 'Cause we might have to lose her."

Then Jeremy smiles at me like he just remembered something.

"Cigarette?" he says, and I smile too. It feels good to have that routine, smoking together, still in place.

"Sounds good," I say, and I press up off the floor. We stand normally—not particularly close, not too far apart, but just like we would have an hour ago, without any leftover intimacy.

Downstairs, Jeremy says, "You know, Sternin, I've begun to really look forward to these bedtime cigarettes."

"Me too," I say, and I wonder what I look like. Jeremy's face is blotchy from crying, and I know mine must be too. I'm wearing a bulky sweater and a scarf. How come boys never seem to feel cold?

"Sternin, I know I don't have to ask you this, so don't be hurt or anything, but please don't talk about it around school, okay?"

"Of course not. It's your family's business, no one else's."

"Thanks, Sternin." Jeremy looks relieved.

"And I won't tell people, you know, that I know about your dad. I know everyone thinks that your parents are divorced."

"Yeah," I say. "That's kind of my fault."

"Yeah?" he says, without any shock or judgment.

"That's what I've always said. That he lives in Arizona."

"Why?"

I shrug. "I guess I thought it would be easier."

"Has it been?"

I exhale until my chest feels hollow. "I guess it used to be."

Jeremy crushes his cigarette and looks like he's thinking very hard. Then he looks back up at me.

"Yeah, but why Arizona?"

I burst out laughing and Jeremy grins at me, proud that he made me laugh. I want to thank him. For making a joke, for not judging my lie, and also for telling me about the cancer because he trusted me with his family's secret and, without even knowing it, helped me figure out my family's.

We don't hug each other good night. Jeremy gives me a kiss on the cheek and gets into a cab. I am suddenly so exhausted. It's like the crying wore me out completely. I fall asleep without any fantasies, and I don't remember any of my dreams when I wake up.

❀❀❀

On Wednesday, Jeremy sits next to me at lunch, and after a few minutes a couple of his friends sit down on his other side. I slouch in my plastic chair. I always watch the cool boys, but I've never gotten to do it this close-up.

"Dude," says Mike Cohen, "Fisher's party is going to be sick."

Mike means Brent Fisher, Marcy's new boyfriend.

"Yeah," says Jeremy.

There's no question whether or not Jeremy is going; even I know that. New York City high schools are so incestuous that if you refused to go to a party that was affiliated in some way with some ex, you'd quickly run out of parties to go to. Besides, a prince is above such trifles. A prince must make his appearance at all the top engagements.

"Where're his parents, anyway?" continues Mike. "Fucking Madagascar?"

"Madrid, idiot," cuts in Ellis White, sitting next to Mike.

"Whatever, man. Fisher's getting a keg."

I don't understand this, since I don't really drink, but I think all high school boys see the availability of a keg as a kind of wide-open treasure chest, all those riches there for the taking. Even Jeremy, who I know gets to sample all the finest wines and mixed drinks at his family's parties, is turned on by the idea.

"Right on, man," Jeremy says, and then Mike looks around Jeremy at me. "You're coming, Sternin, right?"

I didn't even know that he saw me there, sitting on Jeremy's other side. He hadn't acknowledged me till now. I've just taken a bite of my sandwich, so I have some time to chew before answering. I'm excited that whether or not I'm invited isn't a question. I'm Jeremy's friend now, I guess. People have noticed us sitting here almost every day. For all I know, he's told people he comes over to study and for cigarettes, though I'm pretty sure he hasn't.

Luckily, Mike speaks before I can respond. "All right, Sternin. It's gonna be a rage."

I don't know what "It's gonna be a rage" actually means, but I know I can't ask. At least I can tell it's a good thing, so I smile and say, "Sounds awesome," hoping my use of "awesome" isn't too passé.

Peanut butter from my sandwich sticks to the roof of my mouth. I feel so much younger than they are; is this how Kate feels when she hangs out with Jeremy's friends? I can't imagine her ever feeling so awkward. She knows the right things to say.

After Mike and Ellis leave our table, Jeremy turns to me and whispers, "What the hell does 'It's gonna be a rage' mean?" I feel my lips widen into a grin. Jeremy has no idea how happy he's made me.

❋❋❋

Later, when we're smoking, Jeremy interrupts the silence by saying, "You gonna come on Saturday? I just mean, you don't have to if you don't want to."

I'm perched against the planter outside the building. When I straighten up, the stone catches on my sweater and I feel a thread pull. I hope I haven't just ruined the sweater.

"You think I shouldn't?" I ask, disappointed, but then maybe Jeremy knows that I shouldn't, that I wouldn't know what to do at a party like that. He knows better than I if I have any chance of fitting in there. But I want to go, because sometimes I feel like I'm kind of missing out on high school.

"No, of course not, if you want to. I just didn't want you to think you had to come with me. I'm okay, you know—you don't have to babysit me."

I burst out laughing. Jeremy looks hurt.

"I'm sorry, Jer, it's just that . . . God, you'd be the one babysitting me! You go to these parties all the time; it's not like you don't know how to be there."

Jeremy laughs too. "I meant, like, maybe you thought I'd get stupid drunk to drown my sorrows or something."

"Hell, who am I to say that's not what you ought to do?"

"Good point. Maybe drunk is a good thing."

"I've never really drunk much."

"Don't worry, kid, I'll make sure you get good and plastered. Come over before the party and I'll take you there."

"We'll babysit each other," I say, excited that I'm going to the party, thrilled and relieved that Jeremy has volunteered to be my guide.

"Absolutely."

I love that he understood that I wouldn't have wanted to go by myself. I lean back against the planter again, watch Jeremy exhale smoke in the opposite direction. He's always careful not to blow it toward me, like he knows that even though I smoke down here with him, I don't really like cigarettes.

11

Three days later and I'm searching for something to wear to the party. I wonder if Jeremy's family will be there tonight. I've never met his parents. I think Kate will be there. She hasn't been in school for a couple weeks now, and as much as I want to see her, I'm scared too. I know she'll look different. Her hair could be gone by now.

I take care in getting dressed not because I want to look pretty for Jeremy, but because I think I'll be more comfortable at the party if I like the way I look. But I don't want to look overdressed. I mean, it's just a party at someone's house. I know the guys won't be dressed up and the girls won't be dressy so much as slutty, hoping to drag the guys' attention away from the liquor. I wish Jeremy was a girl so I could call him and ask him what he was wearing.

I take a cab down to Jeremy's. I'm not stopped in the lobby, but given a friendly nod from the doorman in the direction of the elevator. It doesn't matter that I don't know the floor, because there's an elevator operator and he does. The mark of a really nice building in New York isn't one where the security is so tight that they don't let you in, but one where they know whether to let you in and take you where you're going without your having to say a word.

The elevator opens directly into the apartment, and I have no idea which way to go. There's no one in sight and the apartment is enormous. I silently narrate my entrance: The peasant girl barely steps inside the castle, scared of the sounds her shoes will make on the marble floor. Will anyone come look for her, or will she be left waiting, standing in the foyer forever? She dares not make a sound until someone comes to acknowledge her. Too frightened—and maybe a bit too stubborn—to move, she stands like a statue, until that's what everyone thinks she is. Days will go by; weeks and months, even. The maids will dust her.

I hear feet shuffling toward me, shaking me out of my nightmare. Kate is walking toward me, sliding her slippers on the floor, in pajama pants and what must be an old T-shirt of Jeremy's, or maybe their father's. I'm relieved to see her—someone to keep me from becoming a statue. And I'm relieved because even though her hair is short, she doesn't look sick. She looks the same.

"Hey, Connelly, you're here."

Now that I've been acknowledged, I can move. I begin with my mouth. "Yup, I'm here."

I think she must be sick of people asking how she's feeling, sicker still of people telling her they like her haircut. So I reach into my purse.

"I brought you a book."

Kate looks surprised. "You did?"

I smile. "It's one of my favorites." I hold the book out toward her. It's my own copy, and I don't think I've ever given a book away before.

Kate flips through it. "It's all underlined."

I smile. "I know. I underlined my favorite parts. You can ignore that."

Kate grins. "Nah, I'll pay attention. Bet I'll be able to tell a lot about you from the parts you marked."

I smile. That sounds like something Jeremy would say.

"Where's your brother?"

"In his room. Come on, I'll show you."

Even though Kate's in slippers and pajamas, I feel underdressed here, like I was supposed to dress more like a grown-up would. My boots—black, pointy-toed, with high heels—clack loudly on the floor, and I consider trying to tiptoe.

"You excited about the party?" Kate asks me as we walk down the hall.

I shrug. "Kind of."

Kate stops walking, and so do I.

"Why are you only 'kind of' excited about the party?"

I bite my lip. "I've never been to a party like this before."

"Don't worry. You'll be the belle of the ball." She starts walking again, but I take a second before I follow her. I kind of can't believe she said that, like maybe she knows about the fairy-tale world too.

Kate opens the door to Jeremy's room without knocking, which I guess is normal for sisters and brothers. Jeremy's room is a mess, and even though I'm such a neat freak, I find the mess comforting.

"Jer-bert, Connelly's here."

"Hey, Con, have a seat," he calls. He must be in the bathroom—his voice comes from behind a door on the other side of the room. Kate climbs onto the unmade bed, and I guess that I'm supposed to sit on the edge of it, next to her. I remain standing. I'm highly aware that I'm a girl and Jeremy, obviously, is not. There are probably things in here that girls aren't supposed to see.

"Ew, Jeremy," Kate calls toward the closed door. "You left your underwear on the floor."

"Oops," Jeremy says, but there's no embarrassment in his voice.

Kate turns to me. "Boys never put anything away."

I shrug. "I wouldn't know."

She pats the bed beside her. "Sit down."

I sit. Kate says, "You look nice. I've never seen you dressed for anything but school."

"Really?" I say, feeling relieved. "I wish you'd been there to tell me that when I was getting ready! I needed some serious advice."

Kate smiles. "Well, you made the right choices."

Kate's said exactly the right thing. And I know she's right, because surely Kate's seen dozens of girls come over here to meet Jeremy before a party, so she knows what she's talking about.

"Hey, Con." Jeremy comes out of the bathroom with jeans and no shirt. He kisses me on the cheek. I really, really hope I'm not blushing.

"I promised you liquor, didn't I? Katie, go get her something."

"No, that's really okay."

"No way, Connie, we had a plan."

Kate's already marched out of the room.

"Where are your parents?" I'm not asking because I'm worried they'll catch us drinking—I can't imagine they care—but because I wonder if Kate will be alone tonight.

"At some dinner thing. They'll be back before we will."

"What about Kate?"

"Our housekeeper's here."

Kate comes in with two bottles of beer in her hand. Nothing fancy, just Bud Light. Jeremy twists off the tops and hands me one, which I begin drinking dutifully. I didn't know you could twist off the tops of these kinds of bottles. I nurse my beer. Jeremy puts on a shirt. Kate climbs back onto his bed and gets under the covers like she's settling in for the night. Jeremy leans down, gives her a kiss, and tosses her the remote.

"No watching scary movies."

Kate wrinkles her nose. "I can watch whatever I want."

"Yeah, but then who gets woken up at three in the morning when someone else can't sleep?"

"You do," Kate says proudly. "But that's totally your job."

"It is?"

"Yeah. Look it up in the Big Brother's Guidebook."

Jeremy grins. "I'll do that, kid. Good night."

"'Night!" Kate calls after us.

In the elevator, Jeremy says, "She likes it better in my room."

"Why?"

"Dunno. Hers has all that medicine in it, but she liked it better in mine before too. I think 'cause it's messier. She'll never make a mess of her own, but she likes mine."

I smile, because I completely understand that.

❀❀❀

Jeremy knows exactly when to arrive at Brent Fisher's so that it's already crowded, but not packed. We settle on a leather couch in what looks like Brent's parents' study and drink beer. The apartment smells like smoke, and someone says that it's a good thing Brent's parents won't be back for a week; it'll give the place time to air out.

"Cole! Sternin!" Mike Cohen calls to us from across the room. "You made it."

Jeremy nods, smiling.

"You want a beer?" he shouts. Jeremy and I hold up our drinks to show that we already have beer.

"Isn't this Fisher's party?" I whisper to Jeremy, feeling cool enough to refer to Brent by his last name.

"Mike Cohen likes to play the host at every party, no matter who's throwing it."

I nod. "I see."

"You'll get used to it," Jeremy says, and I like the implication that this is the first of many of these kinds of parties.

Everyone comes to Jeremy, and since I'm sitting next to him, someone is almost always talking to me too. The beer makes me warm.

I see Brent across the room, leaning in close to kiss Marcy McDonald's neck. Marcy surveys the room, clearly relishing her role as the lady of the house. I glance at Jeremy to see if he's noticed her. I know I'm not his date or anything—it's more that I'm worried he'll be upset to see her. I have a feeling that whatever it is that broke them up has something to do with Kate. It's the only thing I can imagine Jeremy getting that upset about.

Jeremy is looking right at her. He looks at me, quietly angry.

"Do you want another drink?" he asks.

"Sure," I say, even though I know I'm getting drunk and I'm a little worried about how it's going to end up.

"Okay." He takes a breath and stands up, going in the opposite direction from where Brent and Marcy are standing. With any luck, they'll have moved by the time he comes back.

They do move—toward me. Just like that, Marcy is sitting next to me. She perches on the couch, perky and straight-backed. I'm sunk in, my bare arms sweating against the leather. It's like I'm Cinderella, the messy girl covered in soot, and she's one of the prince's other suitors; pristine and poised, light on her feet, bred to be the girl he chooses.

"So, Connelly, you and Jeremy, huh?"

I shouldn't be surprised that she knows my name, even though we've never really been introduced—after all, I know hers—but I am. I try to sit up too, and immediately regret the attempt; I'm settled so deeply into the couch that I have to use the arm of the couch to pull myself up, like I'm such a mess I can't even sit up on my own.

"What?" I say dumbly, so embarrassed by now that I've forgotten what she said.

"He's a good guy. Just, you know, stay on his good side."

Her breath hangs in the air between us, smelling of cigarettes and liquor. I guess mine smells like that too.

"Marcy, I don't know what you mean."

"You'll find out," she says, and makes a big show of crossing her legs and nodding knowingly. I don't want to participate in this conversation, and I think that if I just sit here quietly, she'll go away. With Jeremy gone, no one else is coming over to talk to me.

Now he's coming back. Oh shit. I want to sink into the couch. Actually, I'd prefer that Marcy sink into the couch, all the way in and through to the other side, and then Jeremy can sit right where she's sitting now, hand me my beer, and everything will be fine.

"Hey, Marce," Jeremy says politely.

She looks up at him. "Hiya, Jer."

He hands me my beer and offers her the other.

"No thanks. You know I don't like beer."

"I forgot," he says, but then he takes a swig from the bottle that she just refused, like he'd always planned to keep it for himself. He looks down at her, deliberately but not impolitely, waiting for her to get up and walk away.

She begins to stand. "Listen, Jer, I didn't do anything wrong, okay? I never did anything wrong." And then she walks away, presumably to bitch about us to someone else.

Jeremy sits down next to me. I know he's still not going to tell me what happened between them, but he doesn't have to now. Just knowing that she hurt him is enough to make me hate her too.

"You having fun?" Jeremy asks me.

"Well, the last three minutes notwithstanding—yeah, I'm having a great time." I smile wide, and Jeremy grins back at me.

It's after two when we leave the party. Jeremy is clutching my upper arm. I don't think I'm that drunk, but he seems to feel responsible.

"I really am fine, Jeremy."

"Whatever. I'm walking you home."

We stop outside my building and Jeremy lights us two cigarettes.

"It's nice out."

"No it's not, kid. You're just too drunk to notice how cold it is."

"Am not!"

"Are too!"

I stick my tongue out at him and he grabs me and messes up my hair.

He tosses the butt of his cigarette on the ground.

"Now remember, lots of water, and try to sober up some before you fall asleep."

I nod obediently.

"You're going to have a hell of a headache in the morning," he says, almost apologetically.

"I don't mind," I say cheerfully. I'm such a dork that I'm excited to have a hangover.

"I'll talk to you tomorrow."

"Okay."

He kisses me on the cheek goodbye and walks to the corner. I watch him get into a cab. I don't know exactly how this has happened, but it turns out that Jeremy is the first best friend I've ever had.

12

At school on Monday, I feel like everyone is looking at me differently. I wonder if they think I'm Jeremy Cole's girlfriend, or if that would ever even occur to them—because what would Jeremy be doing, dating me? But I feel like more people are smiling at me in the hallways, rolling their eyes at me when a teacher assigns a last-minute paper, exchanging looks with me in between classes. Something is different, I'm sure of it.

Before first period, Emily Winters comes up to me.

"So what's going on?"

I look at her blankly. I'm sitting on the floor by the lockers, going over our English reading. I know what she's getting at. In a minute I'm going to have to say "just friends," and I'm fine with that, I'm happy about that—but once I say that, the significance with which she's looking at me, the importance she's attaching to me, will go away.

"I heard you went to Fisher's party with Jeremy Cole. I didn't even go!"

I'm not sure what to say. That isn't really a question.

Emily sits down next to me, leans in conspiratorially. "Why didn't you tell me you guys were hanging out?"

What would I have told her? I didn't even know what we were doing at first; whether we were hanging out, how long it would last. There might have been nothing to tell.

Emily continues without waiting for an answer. "So come on, tell me—you guys hooking up or what?"

My hands start to sweat. I don't know how I feel about the fact that people are talking about me. It's strange enough that people I never talked to before are now talking to me. I feign nonchalance. "Emily, no, that's gross—he's a friend." I purposely don't say "just a friend," because the word "just" doesn't feel accurate.

"Honey, ain't nothing gross about Jeremy Cole." I notice for the first time that Emily is actually only trying to sound older and wiser; before, I always felt like she really was.

Nonetheless, I feel my face turning bright red. Not because I have a crush on Jeremy—yes, of course, he's gorgeous and a girl would have to be blind and deaf not to have some kind of crush on him—but it's more than that. There is so much that's private and there's so much I don't want to give away, that I want to keep for just Jeremy and me.

"Dude," Emily says before heading off to class, "it is so not fair not to dish."

I wonder if Emily will spread gossip about us. It doesn't matter, because the gossip she'd spread wouldn't be the truth—the truth is way too complicated for gossip.

❈ ❈ ❈

Jeremy isn't in physics class, and I don't see him at lunchtime. I think something must be wrong—maybe Kate has taken a turn for the worse—and I want to call him. I go so far as to sneak into the nurse's office to use her phone (she never seems to notice that the entire student body uses her phone for personal calls, since we're not allowed to use cell phones in school) when I realize I've never called him before. I don't even have his home number, though it would be easy enough to get it from the class directory, where I imagine he got my number. But I can't imagine calling when he's never actually given me his number—it seems an invasion of privacy. And maybe if there is something wrong, I should wait until I hear from him—he would tell me if he wanted me to know. Maybe I shouldn't assume that whatever it is that's keeping him out of class today is any of my business.

I leave the nurse's office and head back to the cafeteria. I'll grab something and bring it up to the library to eat there. Mike Cohen comes up to me as I'm spreading peanut butter over a bagel.

"Sternin, hey, you seen Jeremy?"

"No, I don't think he's here today."

"Oh, dude. I'll give him a call."

I don't know if I'm supposed to answer that like, Yeah, good idea. How come Mike can just go ahead and call like it's nothing, while I'm completely paralyzed by the possibility?

"Hey," Mike continues. "You know what? Just tell him I was looking for him, okay?"

"Sure." Mike assumes that I'll be talking to Jeremy sometime today, so he needn't call. I feel like I'm lying to him. But I like the way everyone is treating me, now that they know I'm friends with Jeremy Cole. So I don't tell Mike he should go ahead and call Jeremy; I let him think that I'm in a position to convey his message.

And maybe I am; Jeremy will probably still come over for our bedtime cigarettes later.

Mike surprises me by asking, "Do you know—have you seen Kate lately?"

"What?" I say dumbly.

"We were just wondering how she was doing."

"We?"

"You know—the guys and stuff." Maybe Mike Cohen's position as the host of every party makes him the student body ambassador too.

"Oh."

"Have you seen her lately?"

I pause. I guess by now everyone knows that Kate is sick, but maybe they're actually being sensitive about it. Mike sounds genuinely concerned, so I say, "Yeah. I saw her the other night. She's doing okay."

"Thanks. I'll let everyone know."

I nod and smile. I guess one of the nice things about being the prince is that your subjects really do care about you and your family.

❀ ❀ ❀

When I get home, my mother suggests we have dinner together. This doesn't happen often—mostly she leaves me money to order in or I make something for myself, usually ramen or something like it. We go to the diner across the street, where my mother insists on waiting for a booth even though there are plenty of tables with chairs available. When we do finally sit, I order a grilled cheese. It arrives greasy and lukewarm. My mother gets a hamburger. I eat her fries.

"So, how's school?"

"Fine. You know, physics is killing me, but I'm bringing up my grades."

"Hmm."

"Hmm?" I ask.

"Is that Jeremy's help, do you think?" I wonder if this is why she suggested dinner, why she opened the conversation by asking me about school. Maybe she thinks that Jeremy and I are dating but she wants to hear it from me, if for no other reason than to say, "Well, I knew that." It makes me sad, how little she knows me.

"Maybe. He's a good tutor."

"Well, he's more than a tutor."

Here it comes.

"I notice he comes over late at night."

"Oh?"

"Why don't you invite him up? You know, at a more reasonable hour. I could make us dinner."

"You don't cook."

"Sure I cook!"

"When? You never cook."

"I do too; I make chicken and pasta and mashed potatoes."

"Not all at the same time, I hope." I'm laughing, because I can't remember her ever having cooked a meal for me.

"Connelly." My mother puts her hamburger down on its plate and looks at me seriously, and I wonder when this became a serious conversation. It had seemed like I was just teasing her a second ago. "I cook."

"Maybe you used to," I say quietly.

97

"What?"

"Maybe you did a long time ago, when I was little or before I was born, and you just don't realize that you stopped."

She surprises me by considering this. In the silence, something occurs to me, and I surprise myself by asking her, "Did you cook for Dad?"

"For your father?"

"Yes." I can hear the panic in her voice. I don't know why it seemed natural to ask about him now.

"Yes," she answers, speaking slowly, not looking at me. Then she smiles, looking at her plate as she says, "He liked my spaghetti with meat sauce."

She continues before I can answer.

"You liked it too." She looks up at me, smiling. "I have a picture of you eating it. You're covered in tomato sauce."

I should stop asking questions before she gets upset, but I want to know more—even just a little, but more. "If I was covered in tomato sauce, I must have been pretty young in the picture, right?"

"Yes. I guess so."

"So it was when Dad was still alive?" I press.

"I don't remember," she says, and she's looking at her plate again, not at me.

"I think," I say carefully, "that you must have stopped cooking after he died. Maybe you just forgot."

"Maybe," she answers, still not looking at me. When she speaks again, she changes the subject. She looks straight at me and her face is bright: "Will Jeremy be coming over tonight?"

"I don't know." I suspect it's the doormen who've been telling her that it's him—otherwise, how would she know? It could be anyone, for all she knows.

"Well, you can invite him up. We have a terrace, you know."

I shrug.

I find it surprising that she's acknowledging that. we're smoking—the doormen, I guess again—but doesn't seem to mind it. I suppose that the fact that Jeremy is a Cole makes up for his smoking. I wouldn't want Jeremy coming up. Jeremy and I smoke downstairs. But my mother doesn't need to know that I feel that way, especially since I can't explain it. He's been up to study often enough. But the smoking, my coming downstairs, all of that—it's our ritual. Or maybe there's something about having him come up when I'm in my pajamas, ready for bed, that makes me nervous.

We've finished eating. I ask for the check, hoping to speed up our exit; to get back to my room, where Mom usually doesn't bother me. I don't want to talk about Jeremy. I don't want to tell her about our friendship, about Kate's illness, about what I've found out about my father. If it's okay for her to keep something like that a secret from me, then I suppose I've earned the right to keep pretty much anything secret from her.

My mother and I never fight. I can't remember any major fights or childhood temper tantrums. She never assigned me a curfew and I never came home late until the other night, after Brent's party, and then she didn't ask where I'd been. We get along fine this way.

13

"What's your middle name, Connelly?" Jeremy asks me later, when we're smoking. He hasn't explained why he wasn't in school today, and I don't ask.

"My middle name?"

"Yeah. In the handbook, it just says Connelly J. Sternin."

"What's your middle name?"

"I asked you first."

"I asked you second."

"Staddler."

"Jeremy Staddler Cole?"

"Yeah. My mom's maiden name."

"Mine's Jane."

"We have the same initials," Jeremy says, exhaling smoke. "CJS."

"JSC."

"That sounds like the name of a college."

"Oh?"

"Yeah, like . . . Junior Southern College."

"Doesn't sound like it's a particularly good school."

I wrinkle my nose. "Yeah, it's where the students who got rejected everywhere else end up."

Jeremy puts on a fake newscaster voice. "Yes, at JSC we say YES to YOU."

I giggle.

"You know, it's funny, I keep thinking about applying to school next year," he says.

"Well, we know you'll get into JSC."

He smiles. "At least I have my safety all set." He lights a second cigarette, but doesn't offer me one because he knows by now that I only smoke one, and more to keep him company than for anything else. "I just mean . . . I keep thinking about applying. I'm not worried about where I'll go and things, but I just keep thinking about doing the applications."

Well, of course Jeremy isn't worried about where he'll go. Royalty is very well connected. He'll get in wherever he wants.

"I keep thinking about it because everyone around me is worried about it, studying hard for the SATs, going on college visits, calling in favors, all of that. So here's this thing that's still a year away and everyone is thinking about it and so am I, even though it's a year away and I don't want to think that far ahead. But I can't stop."

I wonder for a minute why he's trying to stop himself from thinking so far ahead. I figure it out just as Jeremy explains it.

"So I'm thinking about doing these applications and I'm thinking about whether Kate will be there while I do them."

Jeremy presses at the corners of his eyes with his fingers.

I imagine that in his head he's thinking: She'll be okay. She'll be okay.

"Anyway," he says finally, "I wish everyone would just shut up about them so I could stop thinking that far ahead."

I feel bad. I'm one of those people, obsessing about my grades and the SATs, joining clubs at the last minute so I'll have interesting extracurricular activities on my applications. But Jeremy says, "I don't mean you, Sternin. Just that overall buzz at school."

"I don't think we can do anything about the buzz, Jer."

"I know."

I wait a second before asking: "How is Kate?"

"I don't know. Worse, but I can't tell. She's still just Kate. I'm at school when she's at the hospital, and she's usually home when I get home."

"The school must know—the administration, I mean; they know why she's absent?"

"Yeah, of course they know. Everyone knows. Can't keep a secret at that school."

I nod, thinking of Mike Cohen in the lunchroom.

Jeremy continues, "It's hard enough to keep a secret in this *town*."

"It's okay if everyone knows, Jer; there's nothing you can do about it, so it's okay. They really do care about you, and about Kate."

"I know, but it's just . . . I don't want to accept anyone's support yet. I don't want to worry about being polite and saying the right thing. I just want to hang with Kate."

"Jeremy, I know it's frustrating to think everyone knows your business. I mean, imagine how I felt. We'd never said two words to each other and you knew how my dad died—that my dad died." Jeremy looks apologetic, so I finish the thought quickly; I hadn't meant to make him feel bad. "But it was okay. Because it doesn't really matter that you knew.

"And anyway," I continue, "maybe it was a good thing, because it's why we became friends."

"Sternin, it's not why we're friends."

"No, but it's why you befriended me to begin with." I pause before asking, "Right?"

Jeremy looks guilty.

"It's okay. You thought I might know something—that I might, I don't know, be able to give you advice or something."

"I did. My parents—I should have told you this sooner—they're friends with the doctor who treated your father."

I don't say anything. I wait for Jeremy to explain.

"He was over one night for dinner, giving my parents advice, and he said he thought there was a girl in my class who'd been through it—he said he remembered; he used to work with the guy. Your dad was a doctor, right?"

I nod. That sounds right. I think I've heard that.

"He said it was a real tragic story, the kind you don't forget—" Jeremy stops quickly. "He didn't get into specifics," he says quietly. "He just assumed I must have known your dad had had cancer. Thought I might want to talk to you."

"Oh."

"But really, I promise, I wasn't thinking about it like that. I thought it was a weird thing for him to suggest, really. But then, I don't know. I guess I thought, Maybe there is something she knows, something she could tell me." He pauses and looks straight at me—he's much braver than I am when I've done something I'm ashamed of. "I'm sorry, Sternin. It was rotten."

"It's okay. Really." Jeremy looks so sad, I decide to make a joke. "Hey, I was just glad when I figured it out. I was beginning to think your talking to me was part of some elaborate prank."

Jeremy grins. "Still could be."

"Nah, I know you like me," I say, smiling back, looking straight at him. I know that he likes me, however unlikely that seemed before.

His grin turns sheepish, and he puts his arm around me. "You're a good friend, Connelly Jane." He pats my shoulder.

"So are you, Jeremy Staddler."

"Kate could be gone by the time we get into college."

He says that quickly, and I think it's the first time he's said it out loud. I don't know what to say. I won't agree with him. There are always more treatments, more chances. I'm quiet.

Jeremy's face betrays nothing. We could be talking about the weather.

"I never thought I would wish—I was always looking forward to going to college, and now I just want every day to go at a slow crawl, you know?"

"I understand." But my muscles are tense, like I'm angry at Jeremy. Angry because he's already given up, and I feel like he has no right to.

"It's strange to think you went through this and you don't re-member it."

"I don't know anything about it, Jeremy." Even though I don't agree with him, I want to say something comforting. "But I guess I'm living proof that you survive it."

Jeremy nods. "Yeah, I guess you are." He drops his cigarette to the ground and crushes it with his heel.

"See you tomorrow, CJS." He gives me a kiss on the cheek and hails a cab at the corner. I shuffle back up to my apartment and into my bed. I fall asleep without thinking. In the morning, my alarm surprises me, like I didn't even realize I'd fallen asleep at all. It occurs to me that ever since that night, the night when I found out about the cancer, I've been falling asleep faster. Maybe it's just the fact that Jeremy keeps me up later, so I'm more tired by the time I actually get into bed, or maybe he's keeping my mind busy—I've always fantasized about something or other before I could fall asleep, played a fairy tale in my head to entertain myself. But I haven't for a while now.

❀ ❀ ❀

On Friday, Jeremy invites me over for dinner.

"Just come home with me after school."

I hesitate. "Will your parents be there?"

"Wouldn't you come if they were?"

"Well, yeah, I'm just . . . I'd like to know what I'm getting into." I've never met Jeremy's parents, beyond seeing them at school events. I wouldn't know how to act. Like, before people meet the Queen of England, aren't they schooled in the proper etiquette: the way they're supposed to address her, look at her, that kind of thing?

"My parents will be there. The food will be good. And Kate will sit at the dinner table and look skinny and pale and bald."

My face falls. "Jeremy, that's not fair. You know I don't care—I mean, I care, of course I care. But you know that doesn't make me uncomfortable—except for, you know, being upset that Kate is sick. But you know that that wasn't why I would hesitate to come to your house for dinner—not that I was hesitating, I'd love to come. But you know that I just get nervous—"

"Jesus Christ, Sternin." Jeremy looks hard at me. "I know." And then he launches into his own rambling tirade. "It's okay. I'm just defensive for her; her hair's almost really gone now, and I know she's embarrassed about it. I know you would never look at her like that, but believe me, you might, without even meaning to. Sometimes I find myself looking at her—she just looks so different, and I'm not used to it. But you wouldn't stare at her; I should know that."

"Don't worry about it, Jer."

"Meet me out front after your last class."

❋❋❋

The Coles sit at their dinner table in sweats. Well, not Mrs. Cole, but everyone else. I don't know what I was expecting—that they'd dress for dinner? Jeremy changed into sweats almost as soon as we got there—in his bathroom while I sat on his bed, comfortable now, flipping channels.

I don't see Kate until dinnertime. Jeremy said she was sleeping when we got there. She does look like she's just woken up. She's wearing a scarf wrapped around her head; actually, it's pretty stylish, and would look cute if not for the bags under her eyes, the sallowness around her mouth. I don't think I've ever been in a room with someone so sick before. Except, perhaps, my father, when I was too young to remember.

Jeremy says that on Friday, they order in Chinese food. We sit in the dining room, not the kitchen. The wooden table is glossy beneath our food, and the five of us only take up half of it. The chairs, which are surprisingly comfortable, are covered in what I can tell is very expensive fabric, and I'm scared that I might spill something on it. Usually I douse my Chinese food in soy sauce, but tonight I'm trying to stick to foods I'm least likely to spill. But Kate is sitting across from me, and when she sees my sauceless plate, she says, "Jeremy, pass Connelly the soy sauce." Looking at me, she grins. "It's the best part."

Mrs. Cole says, "Jeremy tells us you've been helping him with his SATs."

I look up from my beef with broccoli, which I'm nearly leaning over the plate to eat. My grandmother always said that I should bring myself to the food, not the other way around, to prevent spilling. Only now do I realize this means that I'm eating without sitting up straight.

"Umm, yes. I mean, it's not like he needs much help."

"You know, we hired him a tutor last year, but he hated it."

Most people I know had SAT tutors. Even I had one, for the math section.

I nod. "Yeah, mine always made me do practice tests." I cringe, thinking that I should have said "yes" instead of "yeah," but I continue: "I felt like I could have done that on my own."

"That's exactly what Jeremy said. And the truth is, he didn't need help with the math, so it was just a matter of vocabulary, that kind of thing."

"That's what Connelly helps me with," Jeremy interjects.

"Connelly," Mrs. Cole says, and I look at her, thinking she's asking me a question, but then I realize she's just considering my name. "It's an unusual name, isn't it?"

"It's my father's mother's maiden name."

"Oh. Irish?"

I shrug. "I guess; I don't honestly know. The rest of my family's Jewish."

"It's an Irish name," Mr. Cole says.

I'm nervous that the conversation might dwell on my family, but instead Mrs. Cole says, "My first name—Joan—was my father's mother's first name. I wish he'd thought of something as interesting as her maiden name instead. I can't even remember what it was—isn't that awful?"

I smile at her.

"And I did the same thing to Kate—my grandmother's name. Parents should be more creative."

"Nah," says Mr. Cole. "Then you'd have kids walking around with ridiculous names." He looks at me. "No offense, Connelly."

"None taken," I say, and I grin, at ease because he teases just like his son.

"You could have named me Staddler instead of Jeremy," Jeremy says.

"No. Your father was set on Jeremy."

"Mom, you were the pregnant one. I think you could have had your way."

Kate speaks up. "She had her way with me. She chose Kate."
She's been quiet all night; I think she must be exhausted, since she
usually talks so easily.

"That's right, I did," Mrs. Cole says, as if, without Kate's having reminded her, she might have forgotten.

I imagine Mr. and Mrs. Cole sixteen years ago, fighting over
what to name their son. Maybe she's lying on her back in bed,
barely able to see over her big tummy, and maybe he's lying with
his hand on her stomach, trying to see if the baby kicks when he
says a particular name, the name he wants. Jeremy. It's such an intimate moment. And here are their kids, talking about it like it's
nothing. Maybe my father fought to name me Connelly. Maybe
my mother doesn't even like the name. I would never ask her how
they ended up choosing Connelly, whether they fought, why my father wanted it. I wonder if my father was especially close with his
mother, and whether this was something he wanted to do for her.

I turn to Mrs. Cole. "Were you close with your grandmother?"

"Oh, I suppose," she replies lightly. "As close as one can be to
someone when there's such a generation gap." I'm disappointed
with her answer. I guess I was hoping she would give me more information, something I could apply to myself somehow. I hope my
father didn't settle on my name as lightly as that.

I'm pleasantly surprised to find that I'm not at all uncomfortable with the Coles. Kate eats her white rice carefully and I can't help
but remember watching Anorexic Alexis eating her food with the
same care, sitting next to Jeremy in the cafeteria, as I am now in his
dining room. When we started staring at Alexis ripping lettuce into
shreds, then picking the shreds up one at a time and chewing them

slowly—I never would have imagined that I'd end up here, with Jeremy, at his home, watching another skinny girl. Kate dips each grain of rice—she eats them one by one—into a pool of soy sauce on her plate. (She's obviously not scared of spilling like I am.)

The Coles eat small portions—all except for Jeremy, who, like most teenage boys, could eat anyone under the table. Mrs. Cole has one helping of rice and one Peking duck pancake. She takes longer than I do to finish, and I think she must be starving by the time we get up from the table.

"Kate," Jeremy says, "want to come watch movies with us?"

She nods, and we settle in the den to watch TV. Kate falls asleep lying across our laps on the couch. I've never, that I can remember, had someone lie on me while sleeping, and Kate's weight across my thighs is warm. We're watching our second movie when Jeremy's parents stick their heads in to say good night, and his father lifts Kate off the couch to take her to her bedroom. I feel her absence on my legs. The Coles, extraordinary though their circumstances may be—the money, the ill daughter, etc.—seem the picture of a family to me. Like something out of a storybook.

Jeremy surprises me by coming home with me and lighting up outside my lobby like usual.

"You know, my mother said we could smoke upstairs."

"God, my mom would go nuts."

"Well, I think the thrill of having a Cole regularly at the house . . ."

"Shut up." It's the first time I've said anything to him about his royalty, his social status compared to mine. Jeremy and I grin at each other. I bring my cigarette to my lips.

"Jesus Christ, Sternin, you barely inhale."

"Hey, I'm here for the company, not the nicotine."

Jeremy begins to laugh, but his smile drops abruptly and he presses his temples with the thumb and middle finger of his left hand. "Thanks for coming to dinner."

"My pleasure."

"I mean it; it was nice having you there."

I smile, and Jeremy smiles back at me.

While I'm getting ready for bed, I feel like there's something terrible I've done, but I can't remember what. Like I said something wrong at dinner, or stole an ashtray or something.

It's awful, but I'm jealous of Jeremy. It's so wrong to be jealous of someone when the person he loves most in the world is so sick, but I'm jealous of him for having Kate to love. I'm jealous of the way that his parents said good night to us, and I'm jealous of Kate's legs across his lap. Worst of all, I'm grateful for Kate's illness. Without it, Jeremy and I wouldn't be friends.

I get out of bed, walk over to my bookshelves. Without turning on the light, I locate my copy of *A Farewell to Arms*, open it to where I'd stuck that picture of my parents. In the darkness, I can just make out their shapes. I wonder if this is what Jeremy's parents looked like when they were that age. I put the picture back, put the book back on its shelf, get back into bed.

I remember how empty my lap felt when Kate was put to bed. I imagine Jeremy walking around with that emptiness every day for the rest of his life.

And I'm still jealous.

14

On Saturday, I wake up frantic, my skin itching. Why haven't I figured it out yet? How much longer will I walk around without knowing the truth about my father?

Jeremy comes over in the afternoon to help me cram for the physics midterm on Monday. My mother's not home, and for a change we sit in the living room, textbooks spread out on the coffee table. Jeremy's up on the couch. I'm down on the floor, my legs under the table, and I'm trying to work on the vector problem in front of me, but I can't concentrate.

"Sternin. Dude."

I blink. "Huh?"

"You've been staring at that problem for hours. Do you want me to walk you through it?"

I look down at the textbook. I actually know how to do this problem. That's not why I haven't finished it.

"Sternin?"

I look back up at Jeremy.

"I can't concentrate."

"I can tell."

How come Jeremy can concentrate when his sister is so sick and I can't concentrate when my father has been dead for years?

"Sternin?"

"I'm sorry, Jeremy. It's very nice of you to be here helping me, but I'm not paying any attention. You must have somewhere else . . ." I trail off, because I think he knows what I'm thinking: Why waste any time here with me when you could be soaking up time with Kate?

"I don't want to go home, Sternin. It's too hard to be there sometimes."

"Oh," I say. Maybe physics is actually an escape for Jeremy, time off from thinking about Kate.

"We can take a break," he offers.

"It's hardly a break when I haven't been working."

"Well, let's just give up on the illusion, then." He reaches for the remote and starts flipping channels.

There's a reason Jeremy's my first best friend. He's the first person I've been friends with where there wasn't this lie about my parents. It's been so stupidly nice not to have to worry about slipping up; not to have to keep him away so that he won't get too close, figure out my parents weren't divorced, see something he wasn't supposed to. With everyone else, I was so intent on maintaining the story that I never had a chance to think about finding out the truth. He's the reason I'm going to find out. I want to tell him the whole story. I want just this one relationship, this one friendship, to be real.

"Jer?"

"Hmm?"

"Mute the TV for a second."

"What's up?" he asks, putting the remote down.

I slide up onto the couch beside him. "I know you befriended me because you thought I knew about losing someone to cancer."

"Sternin, we've been over this—"

"No, it's okay. I don't mind—we're good friends now." I take a deep breath. Even now, saying that makes me happy.

I continue: "But I can't help you."

"I know, Sternin. You were so young when your dad died."

"No, Jeremy, there's more to it." I pause. "I didn't know my father had cancer until you told me."

Jeremy looks at me like I'm crazy. "I don't understand."

"I pretended that I'd known. But my family never told me. I don't know . . . I never knew how he died."

"Why didn't your mother tell you?"

"I'm not sure."

"Haven't you asked?"

I don't answer right away. I don't want to lie, so I say, "Maybe, when I was younger . . . I think I always understood that she couldn't tell me." I can remember the exact age I was when that became clear, the exact day. Just turned eight years old, just started third grade.

"Why on earth would she want to keep that from you?"

"I'm not sure."

"Is that why you lied?" he asks. "Is that why you told everyone your parents were divorced?"

"Yeah. It seemed easier. That way, no one would ask questions I wouldn't know the answers to. I could just make up the answers."

"And never have to worry about finding out the truth."

"Until now. This is the weirdest part—now I want to find out."

"Why is that the weirdest part?"

I purse my lips and then try to explain. "Ever since that night when you told me you knew my father was dead—ever since then, I can't explain it, I've needed to know. I've been so curious. Like, physically curious—like, it's hard to sit still in my bedroom if I know there might be some clue in the living room that I haven't looked for yet. Uncomfortably curious."

Jeremy shakes his head. "But, Connelly, that's not strange."

"Why not?"

"I guess I think it's stranger that you never looked before."

This almost makes me laugh. Is it really more unnatural that I've never been curious before than it is to be filled with this alien sensation? Would it have been normal to be filled with it all my life?

"I never needed to know before." I mean that my body needs to know, that my body actually won't let me relax until I know.

"But I've told you about the cancer, so now you know. Why are you still trying to find things out? You have your answers."

I shake my head. "No. I don't."

Jeremy speaks with certainty. "But it was cancer, I know it. I told you—the oncologist."

"No, there's more to it. You said that he said it was a tragic story."

"I think he meant because of you—you know, a young daughter." Jeremy's uncomfortable, I can see, adding that last part.

"No, he's a cancer doctor. He must see that all the time. There must be something more, don't you see?"

Jeremy considers this, and I look straight at him as I continue.

"I don't think cancer killed him. Or at least not the cancer alone. There's something else that makes it worse. I just have no idea—I can't even make something up about it."

Jeremy grins at me. "And we all know that Connelly has an oh-so-active imagination."

I blush. I don't know whether Jeremy is joking or if he realizes how true this is. This is the first time in my life that I've had so many real things going on, so many things I can't fantasize my way away from, or out of.

Jeremy continues, serious now. "Maybe your mom thought you were too young to know about death and then, by the time you were older, it seemed like—I don't know, like she'd gone this long without telling you, so why bring it up?"

"I think there's something more to it. Think about it, Jeremy—there are no pictures of him up in my apartment. My mother's mother won't even talk about him. His own parents don't talk about him—like about when he was young, old stories. It's like they're mad at him."

"Maybe they're angry at him for leaving them. I've read about that, the stages of grief and all that stuff."

I shake my head. "No. It's been too long. They wouldn't be angry at him for that anymore. Certainly not all of them." I pause. "It's not anger. She's, they're—scared to talk about him. It feels like something about his death was humiliating, and something about it was, I don't know, worse."

I hope Jeremy doesn't think I mean that my father's death was worse than mere cancer. Mere cancer is what's hurting his sister, and I don't mean that my father's death was worse for my family than hers would be for his. But Jeremy doesn't seem to interpret it that way. He's still thinking of my family, not his.

"Connie, that doesn't make sense."

I don't say anything, and Jeremy opens his mouth like he's going to tell me I'm wrong again. Then he shuts it. I wonder if he's conceding the point because I've convinced him, or because he just realized that it's not his place to argue.

"I'm sorry you had to find out like that," he says. "About the cancer, I mean."

"I'm sure it never occurred to you that I didn't know."

"No. But it should have."

I open my mouth to protest, but he stops me. "No, Sternin. I come from a family where everyone talks about everything—talks too much, if you ask me. I didn't even think that yours might be a different kind of family. One where you don't talk about things like that. It was selfish of me not to think past myself."

I shrug. "Don't worry about it. Really," I add when he looks like he doesn't believe me. "Anyway, I'm happy I know. Well, I mean, 'happy' isn't the right word."

"I know what you mean."

I smile at him. "Okay. Thanks."

"It's funny, though. You'd think she'd—I don't know." Jeremy thinks for a minute, stretching his long legs out in front of him, crossing them at the ankles. "I don't know, that she'd have made something up or something. So you'd know—something. Or at least, I mean, why not tell you about the cancer? Then you wouldn't be searching for some other . . . some bigger thing."

I consider this, then shake my head. "No, I don't think she would."

"Why not?"

I wait to answer, doing with my body the opposite of what Jeremy is doing with his: curling my arms around my legs, making myself small, resting my chin on my knees. I look at my feet. "I haven't given her any reason to make something up. She'd only have to do that if I insisted on knowing, if I asked questions, and I haven't. I made up a lie so that I wouldn't have to ask her, so that the truth wouldn't even matter." I look up at Jeremy. "Plus, I don't think she'd want to lie to me about it. I think she'd prefer this to having told me a lie."

Jeremy leans forward, considering what I've said. "There's something kind of nice about that—your mom not wanting to lie to you."

I nod. "I know. But I need to know the truth now."

"I understand. I'll help you, if I can."

I smile. "I know you will."

Jeremy sits back again. "Thank you for telling me. I'm glad you feel like . . . I don't know, that you can trust me."

And Jeremy and I smile at each other, and finally I'm able to pick up my physics textbook and complete the problem I'd been staring at for so long. We work for the rest of the day, and Jeremy says he'll take me out to celebrate if I get higher than an 86.

When I get a 95, we decide it has to be a major celebration. We invite Kate out for ice cream sundaes.

❋ ❋ ❋

I'm standing in the Coles' foyer again. It's very different from the first time—I feel comfortable here now; there's no chance I'll be forgotten or ignored. I could have walked all the way inside if no one had been here to greet me. But that's not what has happened today. Today I'm still in the foyer because I'm waiting to leave, and I'm working up a sweat under my winter coat. Kate is still getting ready because a few minutes ago, Mrs. Cole saw the three of us waiting for the elevator and said that Kate wasn't dressed warmly enough. Kate didn't like the coat Mrs. Cole wanted her to wear. So they disappeared into Kate's room to negotiate what she'd been wearing underneath the lighter coat. Jeremy trotted after them. And so I'm waiting by the elevator.

Mr. Cole walks by and sees me.

"Connelly, how are you?"

"Fine. How are you?"

"Very fine indeed. You waiting for Kate?"

"Yup."

"Yeah, sorry about that. She's become pretty picky about what she wears since she lost her hair—I mean . . ." He seems flustered suddenly, to have said it so simply. I feel sorry for him and interrupt.

"Hey, twelve-year-old girls can be very stubborn about their sense of style," I say, as though I don't know that this is a bigger deal than that. But he seems to appreciate my feigned ignorance.

"Exactly." He smiles at me. "Well, I'm sure they won't be much longer. You might want to settle in, take off your coat, grab some provisions from the kitchen—just in case you end up camped out here, you know."

I laugh at his joke and he moves past me, and I'm alone in the foyer again. I hear Kate yell, "No I won't!" and I wonder what's happened. She and Jeremy are walking toward me, Kate's face obviously red from crying, but she's wearing the same clothes she'd been wearing earlier.

"Come on, let's get going," Jeremy says. I press for the elevator.

Jeremy insists on taking a cab, even though the restaurant is just a few blocks away. I see that even though he's allied himself with Kate in this fight, he's worried about her getting cold too, and wants to spend as little time as possible outdoors.

It's awkward in the cab. None of us says anything. Everything I can think of to say has to do with Kate's outfit—like, Great coat; cute boots.

"What kind of sundae you gonna get, Connie?" Jeremy asks finally.

"I haven't decided."

"No fun. I know exactly what Kate's getting." The cab arrives, and Jeremy pays the driver, and Kate and I scoot out and into the restaurant. Kate doesn't take the bait, doesn't respond to her brother's teasing her about her order. She stays silent, still angry at her mom. You'd think she was being a brat if you didn't know the whole story.

Jeremy continues as we're led to the table, ignoring the serious turn this outing has taken, still trying to joke. "Kate always gets scoops of chocolate, vanilla, strawberry, and coffee, with hot fudge, nuts, and whipped cream, and then swirls it all together until it is a very, very disgusting shade of dark pink."

"God, Kate," I say, trying to get in on the joke. "Can you eat all that?"

"Yes!" she says defensively.

"Well," I continue, desperate to say something right, "I'll be full after two bites. My eyes are much bigger than my stomach."

"How about you, Jeremy?" I ask as we sit down. "What are you gonna get?"

"Hey, I'm on your side—I can't finish one of those huge things. Want to split something?"

"Perfect."

We split a hot fudge sundae. Kate's sundae comes and she does in fact swirl it all together, and it does turn a gross color, and she does begin slurping it up, but after a few spoonfuls she loses interest. I wish Jeremy and I had never suggested this outing of ours. Kate looks like she's about to cry. I nudge Jeremy, who's up to his elbows in our sundae. He looks at his sister.

"Kate?" he says quietly.

"I don't think I can eat this," she says. She's staring at the sundae as though finishing it is a matter of life and death: finish it and prove you're the same girl you used to be; don't finish it and admit just how sick you really are.

"That's okay," Jeremy says firmly. "It doesn't matter."

"Yes it does," Kate says, and a couple of tears slip down her cheeks.

I hate how important the sundae has become. It feels intensely like this could be the last time Kate will ever come here, like it might be the last time she'll ever turn a sundae pink, the way she's been doing since she was a little girl. This place will never be the same for her, no matter what happens with her illness. When Jeremy and I go back to my place later, he chain-smokes on my terrace, almost a whole pack of cigarettes. I've never seen him so upset, and I feel awful that I was the reason for it. My stupid physics score prompted the whole thing.

15

My mother and I don't look alike. I'm always fascinated when you see parents with their children and their relationship is very obvious. The Coles are obviously related. Just take one look at Jeremy's mother and you can tell where he got his eyes, his mouth, and his hair. His hands match his father's. Kate's chin and lips match her brother's.

But it's more than that, more than just the way that they look. Kate makes the same gestures as Jeremy when she speaks, has the same spark in her eye when she's teasing her brother that her brother has when he's teasing me. When I call Jeremy's house and his father picks up, he always makes small talk before passing the phone to his son, and when he asks how school is and how my day was, I can hear the same intonations that are in Jeremy's voice when he asks those questions.

I wonder if my mother and I share traits like that. The kind that you pick up from living with the same person for a long time. I must have something of my mother's, some habit, like the way she makes little swishing noises with her lips when she's walking around the apartment, looking for a lost pair of shoes. But I've never noticed myself doing that. Technically, I guess it's an unconscious habit, but still. I've lived with her all my life. I don't question why we don't look alike—that's just some trick of genetics—but I do wonder what traits of hers I may have picked up over the years.

❊ ❊ ❊

I start going to the Coles' after school; Jeremy and I are still studying together and he likes us to go to his apartment now, not mine. Neither of us would ever say the reason, but of course it's to spend more time with Kate.

Last week, Jeremy's cell phone rang around nine. Kate and I were eating ice cream on the couch, eavesdropping.

"Hey, Fisher, what's up?"

Kate and I could hear Brent Fisher screaming through the phone; he was someplace noisy.

"No way! I've been dying to go there!"

Brent screamed some more.

"Tonight?" Jeremy stood up, looked back at Kate and me on the couch, then headed for the door, holding the phone. "No, man," we could hear him say as he left the room. "Nah, not tonight."

Kate waited until we couldn't hear Jeremy anymore and said, "He doesn't go out like he used to." She sounded like she felt guilty.

"I know. But it's not your fault."

"Sure it's my fault," she said, almost shrugging.

"Not any more than it's mine," I said, wanting to make a joke. "Seriously, the minute your brother decided to hang out with me must have also been the minute he gave up going to lots of parties. I am not a party girl."

Kate giggled. "I guess you're not."

"Hey," I said, feigning offense, "I could go to plenty of parties if I wanted."

"Yeah, but you don't really want to."

"Once in a while," I said honestly.

"Once in a while," Kate echoed thoughtfully. Then she said, "It's just . . . he used to have so much fun all the time. It used to be important."

"What do you mean, 'it used to be important'?"

Kate shoved her ice cream bowl onto the coffee table; we both ignored that it was mostly full.

"I mean, *he* used to be important. Whether or not he went to these parties was important. It mattered. People wanted him to be there."

"They still do—they still always invite him."

"But it's not the same now."

I thought about this. Kate was right; it did used to matter—a party wasn't a party unless Jeremy Cole was there. You weren't cool unless the prince validated your party with his presence. And Kate understood that.

"You know," I said slowly, "I had this theory about your brother, about high school."

Kate looked intrigued now, excited. "What?"

I was excited too. I was going to tell Kate something I'd never told anyone. I leaned in conspiratorially. "That the school was like a kingdom, and that Jeremy was, like, Prince Charming, and everyone else—"

Kate cut me off. "Like in a fairy tale. Like the girls wanted to be Cinderella, or Sleeping Beauty."

"Exactly!" It was exciting—it was *fun*—confiding this to Kate. Maybe making all this stuff up in my head didn't mean I was weird, or crazy.

"That makes perfect sense!" Kate said, almost shouting. "Jeremy is totally the prince at school. Like, at parties, girls want to spend time with him, just like Cinderella at the ball."

"Oh my God, exactly! That's totally what I thought too." Kate and I grinned at each other.

A moment later, though, Kate leaned back on the couch, turning quiet. "Is he still the prince, even if he's not there?"

I nodded solemnly. "Yes, he's still the prince. Royalty is something you're born with. Like when Sleeping Beauty was hidden in her castle, asleep, she was still a princess, even if she wasn't going to balls and holding court."

"That's right."

"Yeah."

Kate smiled then, like she'd just figured something out. "That's like me, then. Sleeping Beauty. 'Cause if Jeremy's a prince, then I'm a princess, huh?"

I never thought anyone else would find sense—would find comfort—in my fairy-tale world.

"Absolutely," I agreed.

"Yeah." She nodded, and we both smiled, sitting close.

❖ ❖ ❖

Tonight, the three of us are in the den: Kate is reading the book I gave her, Jeremy is taking a practice SAT, and I'm reading about the current situation in the Middle East for my Conflicts class. None of us is paying particularly close attention, though, because the TV is on in the background. Kate's face is swollen from the chemo-therapy; her cheeks are pudgy—grotesquely chubby, making a joke of what a healthy face is supposed to look like; not at all like cheeks that make you want to squeeze them. Jeremy makes a joke of it; calls her a chipmunk, storing nuts in her cheeks for the winter.

Jeremy's phone rings and he picks it up, then gets up from his chair and goes into the other room. I put my reading down and turn to Kate.

"How are you liking the book?"

"The writing is better than the story."

"I thought the same thing when I read it. But I loved the main character."

"Yeah, me too." She smiles at me. "I like the parts you under-lined."

"Thanks," I say, because what she says sounds like a compliment.

Kate pauses, and then she says, "Did you read this in school, when you were in seventh grade?"

I shake my head. "I just read it for fun."

"'Cause I thought maybe the teachers might have asked you to bring me my homework or something, like, Oh, Connelly, we hear you're spending time with the Coles. Bring this to Kate Cole so she can catch up. Like they don't realize I might not come back—or anyway, not anytime soon."

I know I shouldn't, but I can't help myself: I giggle.

"What's funny?"

"I'm sorry, I just never thought of your name as Kate Cole be-fore. It just sounds—"

Kate interrupts me. "I know! Like the nursery rhyme! You'd think my parents would have thought of that before naming me. But they were thinking Katherine Cole; they didn't stop to think about the nickname. So stupid."

"Yeah."

"And the worst is my middle name. Ann. Katherine Ann Cole. So boring."

"My middle name is Jane; can't get much more boring than that."

"Yeah, but at least your first name is interesting."

"Except I hate when people shorten it to Connie. It sounds like I should be wearing white tights and clogs when I hear that."

"Jeremy calls you Connie."

"Yeah, but he's not people."

Kate grins at me, and I blush. I think Kate likes to make me blush.

"Anyway," she says, "I was just wondering if this was on some teacher's reading list. They keep sending e-mails letting me know what to study so I don't fall behind. I ignore them, so maybe they thought they could go through you."

"Nope. I just gave you the book because I love it."

"Oh. Well, thank you. I really do like it."

I smile and turn back to my homework, but then Kate says, "Can you believe they knew before I did?"

"What?" I say dumbly.

"The teachers. My parents told the school about the cancer before they told me. They just told me I was sick, that they were running tests. But they knew what it was." She sounds angry.

"Maybe they were just—"

"Protecting me? That's what Jeremy says, but that's a stupid idea of what's protection. As if it wasn't scarier going to the hospital without knowing why. I thought I had some rare, horrible disease that the doctors had never heard of and that they wouldn't know how to fix me."

"That's terrible."

"Jeremy was the one who got them to tell me. I heard them fighting about it."

It's strange; I've never imagined Jeremy fighting with his parents. I wonder what it's like—it must involve yelling, or something like yelling, if Kate overheard them.

"When they finally did tell me, they didn't tell me the truth."

"What do you mean?"

"They didn't tell me how bad it was—they said 'leukemia,' but they didn't tell me how bad it was. Like they didn't think I could just go Google it or something."

I don't know what to say. She seems so calm.

"So I asked Jeremy, and he told me the rest of it. He told me what the prognosis was. He told me what the real chances were. They didn't."

I think about my mother, about the things she's kept from me. But then, I'm a liar too.

I ask Kate, "Were you angry at them?"

Kate shrugs. "I'm not sure. I don't think so. I think I was just— I don't know. I know they thought they were protecting me, but didn't they know that keeping me in the dark made it so much scarier?"

I pause, and then I say, "Maybe they weren't trying to protect you. Maybe they were actually protecting themselves. Like they just couldn't face having to tell you that."

Kate thinks about this for a minute, and so do I.

Kate speaks first. "I don't know. That's so . . ." She seems to be searching for the word. "Weak," she says finally, sounding disappointed.

"Yeah. And I wasn't trying to defend them—I was just trying to understand."

"I know," Kate answers, but I can tell there's more she wants to say.

"What is it?" I ask.

"I want to ask you something, but it's private."

I smile. "You can ask me anything—really, I don't mind." And I don't; I don't think there's anything I can't talk to Kate about.

Kate bites her lip. "Did your parents do any better—when your dad was sick?"

It takes me a minute to figure out what to say, but I smile at Kate to let her know I'm not upset that she's asked.

"No," I say finally. "They didn't do any better."

"Maybe all parents suck at telling their kids things."

I smile. "Maybe. But I was so young; it's different."

"How?"

"I was two. Even if they told me, I wouldn't have known what cancer was."

"So what happened when your mom did tell you?"

I'm not scared to tell Kate. If anyone can understand what it's like not to know something important, it's her.

"She didn't."

"What?"

"No one ever told me how he died."

Kate's eyes go wide. "No one told you?"

I shake my head.

"So how did you find out?"

I blush. "Your brother. He let it slip when . . ."

"When he told you about me," Kate finishes for me.

"Yeah."

"That must have been so embarrassing."

I look straight at Kate now. "Yes!" I say emphatically, kind of excitedly. "Yes, it really was."

Jeremy comes in then. Kate looks at me and I know she's not going to tell him what I've told her, because she doesn't know whether I've told him about my dad.

"Who was on the phone, Jer?" she asks, and I'm glad she does because I never could. But as his sister, she has every right to invade his privacy.

"Mike Cohen. Spreading gossip as usual."

"Funny," I say. "You don't generally think of boys as being gossips."

"Sternin, boys are the worst gossips, believe me."

"So what's the gossip?" Kate asks.

"Brent Fisher and Marcy McDonald are breaking up."

Kate makes a face like she's tasted something sour. "Ugh. Marcy."

"I know, kid. Serves her right."

"Jesus Christ," I say, feeling left out. "One of these days, one of you is going to have to tell me what happened with Marcy McDonald!"

Kate grins at me. "One of these days, one of us will."

"Good comeback, kiddo," Jeremy says approvingly.

"Are you kidding?" I groan. "She's full of them. Kate always knows the right thing to say."

"Anyway," Kate says, "Brent's a nice guy. Hope he's the one who dumped her."

"Kate," Jeremy mock-admonishes. "I don't like this nasty side of you."

"Got it from you, big brother," Kate says, and Jeremy pounces on her, gently and very carefully play-wrestling, and Kate dissolves into giggles. I allow myself a jealous glance at them and then go back to my Middle East reading.

❋ ❋ ❋

We ride silently to my building. Jeremy always takes me home so we can share a couple of bedtime cigarettes. We almost never talk in the cab, so tonight's silence doesn't have any big implications. I'm thinking about Kate—about her family, being foolish enough to think that they might get away without telling her the truth about her disease, without even telling her that she had cancer at all. What did they think—that she wouldn't figure it out when the chemo made her hair fall out? What did they say to the doctors to make them not insist upon telling her? That they would tell their daughter when the time was right, some other time, like maybe after this whole thing had blown over, which surely it would?

And I think about what Kate said, that her parents were weak not to tell her, no matter how hard it might have been for them. I think about my mother and me, the care we take to avoid confrontation, be it about my father, or about what I do every day after school with the Coles, or why I came home so late that Saturday night. My mother doesn't ask. Tit for tat—I don't ask, so she doesn't either.

Weak, Kate called it. I never thought of my mother that way, but then, I did think that I had to be strong, strong enough to protect her from my questions. Like by inventing a deadbeat dad sunbathing in the desert, I could protect her from the truth. But she's the one who knows who my dad really was, and I'm the one in the dark.

I'm sick of thinking about this. I want to think about something else, anything else. I think about Jeremy and Marcy McDonald. By the time we reach my block, I've built up quite a curiosity.

Outside my building, cigarette in hand, my curiosity gets the better of me.

"Are you ever going to tell me what happened with Marcy McDonald?"

Jeremy's surprise is written on his face. I think he wonders why I even care.

"I'm sorry, Jer. I just . . . I just really want to know."

"Why?"

"I don't know. Maybe I'm just being girly or something. I just want to know."

"I promised Kate I'd never tell."

"Kate?"

He breaks his gaze; looks above me, behind me. "Yeah. She was embarrassed. I promised her."

He still isn't looking at me, so I hold the sleeve of his shirt. "Okay. I understand."

"Okay." Jeremy takes a last drag and flicks the cigarette onto the ground. "See you tomorrow," he says, and heads toward the corner.

"Are you mad at me?" I say to his back. The possibility scares the absolute crap out of me.

Jeremy turns around. "Mad?"

"Yeah. For asking."

Jeremy grins at me and without stepping any closer says, "Sternin, you got a lot to learn about me still, huh?"

I exhale. I hadn't even realized I'd been holding my breath. I feel better and turn to walk into the lobby.

16

On Thursday, a couple of weeks before winter break, Jeremy tells me to meet him in the library at lunch.

"What for?"

"I have an idea," he says mysteriously. I think this must be some kind of prank that his friends want to pull and they need me as an accomplice. The teachers would never suspect me.

They redid the library recently, so it doesn't have that old-book smell you'd expect. It feels like there are more computers here than books. I manage to find a table entirely surrounded by bookshelves, except for one side that's up against a window. I'm reading when Jeremy taps my shoulder.

"What's this all about?"

"Okay." Jeremy looks ridiculously excited. "Don't take this the wrong way. Okay. If you don't like this idea, I promise not to bring it up again."

"Okay," I say warily.

"I'm sure I can find things out for you."

I look at him blankly. I have no idea what he's talking about. My cluelessness must be written on my face, because Jeremy says, "About your father, I mean."

"What about my father?" I say, still dumb.

"About his . . . about what happened to him. I'm sure I can find out more for you. From the oncologist, maybe."

I look hard at Jeremy. Part of me is angry. It will be easier for him to find out than it has been for me.

But Jeremy's right: he can find things out for me. What's more important to me—knowing the truth, or the way I find the truth? I'm not really sure what my answer is, actually. Because all this has to do with how I feel about the truth having been kept from me. How I feel about being left in the dark regarding the death of my own father, about my family.

So I have a decision to make. Do I want to find out because I'm ashamed that I don't know, or do I want to find out because I just have to know? I think I need to know. I'll take Jeremy's help. He can ask questions I can't ask. If nothing else, he'll get me that much closer.

"Sternin?" I've been quiet for a few seconds, considering. Jeremy must think I'm mad, because he continues, "Only if you want me to. If you want me to stay out of it, I promise I won't ever bring it up again—"

I interrupt: "No, Jer. It's a good idea. You're right."

"I'm right?"

"You might be able to find something out. You already knew more than I did." He nods. "At least, maybe you can find something out from the oncologist, get him to draw a comparison between your father and Kate."

I immediately wish I hadn't said this, but Jeremy enthusiastically agrees. "Exactly. I figured I could say, Remember that girl you mentioned, the one whose dad had leukemia like Kate? Let on that

I think that's how he died, and so I'm upset about Kate, having the same kind of sick, and play on the doctor's sympathy—"

I look at Jeremy, my eyes wide. I can't believe he just said that.

"Listen, Sternin," he says, "I'm sorry, but I could use the distraction. It'd be nice for the cancer to be about something else, just for a while."

"Okay," I say, and nod. And I completely understand what he means. For me, investing myself in Jeremy's life and family has been a distraction from my situation, so I can't blame him for using my situation to distract him from his. At least he's being honest about it. That's more than I can say for myself.

Turns out, the oncologist, the Coles' dear family friend, Dr. Graham Kleinbaum, is having dinner at the Coles' next Wednesday. He's not Kate's doctor, because the Coles wanted a pediatric specialist, but Jeremy says his parents pretty much look to him before making any decisions about Kate's treatment. In the last few weeks, there's been some talk about a bone marrow transplant for Kate.

At first I think Jeremy is going to invite me over for dinner that night. I have dinner there all the time as it is; it wouldn't be odd or anything if I was there. But he doesn't, and I'm relieved. First of all, I don't think Jeremy would be able to ask the doctor questions about my father if I was there, and second of all, I don't know how I would be able to stop myself from asking questions, and that would be the worst humiliation of all—interrogating my father's oncologist in front of the Coles. What if he remembered who I was and just started talking about it on his own, expecting that I would know about my father's disease and I'd have to play dumb—or actually, play smart, pretending to know more than I do?

Jeremy comes over late on Wednesday. I pull on my coat and rush downstairs. I don't know what I think I'm going to learn, since I'm so sure my father didn't die of cancer after all, but I'm anxious, and the elevator has never seemed so slow. It's freezing out, and the air is so dry I know my sheets will crackle with static electricity later. Jeremy's hands are shoved in his pockets and his cigarette dangles precariously between his lips. We stand close. Jeremy promised me the play-by-play, but I just want to hear how it all ended—what he found out.

"We're definitely moving forward with the bone marrow," he begins, without saying hello or even giving me a cigarette.

"What?"

"The bone marrow. I go to get tested to see if I'm a match tomorrow."

"Oh. Okay." I'm a little put out that he's opening with this instead of with my father. I know it's selfish, but I can't help it.

"I'm nervous, though. I mean, I hope I'm a match, of course, but . . ." Jeremy's voice trails off, and it looks like he's about to cry. "My parents are so excited. They're sure I'll be a match; they're sure this step is all that Kate needs. I don't want to disappoint them. But I'm so scared.

"Isn't that awful? I mean, of course I want to be a match and of course I don't care what they have to do to me to get the marrow out for Kate. But I'm still so scared of how much it'll hurt. God."

I don't know what to say. I mean, I would be scared too, but it's strange to see Jeremy acting so frightened. Jeremy covers his eyes with the heels of his hands. I can see he's pressing hard. I don't know how to change the subject to my father.

"What else did the doctor say?" I ask, and when Jeremy looks at me, hard, I add, "About the procedure?"

"I don't know. I stopped listening. He was talking percentages, success rates. I was getting angry, kind of, like, he was getting us so excited about this and at the same time he was telling us that there's such a small chance it'll even work. They're so determined. My mother—like when she's planning a party for one of her charities and everything's up in the air and the caterer's canceled and the tickets aren't selling, she always knows how to get everything right so that it's perfect on party night. She loves solving problems, getting all the answers. Like this is no different from that."

"Well, maybe it isn't." Jeremy looks at me, shocked. "I just mean, well, I figure the doctor knows better than the rest of us. He's supposed to be the best." And then I see an opportunity to steer the conversation back to me, and even though I know I shouldn't be so selfish, I say, "I'm sure that's why my family chose him." Without a cigarette, I can crush my hands into fists inside my pockets.

"Huh?"

"Why my parents went to him—to Dr. Kleinbaum, for my dad."

Jeremy blinks. "Of course," he says, and it's like he's remembered his manners, or remembered I'm there, or something. "I didn't get anything about your dad, Sternin."

"What?" I spit the word out hotly, watch the cloud that my breath makes.

"He didn't tell me anything."

"Did you ask?"

"Yes, but he said he couldn't tell me anything."

"Didn't he say anything?"

"No."

"Well, tell me what the conversation was."

"I'm so tired, Sternin," he says, and I can tell he's expecting me to stop talking about my father—to reach out to him, give him a hug, rub his back, tell him it will be okay. But I don't; I'm still thinking about my father. I'm still waiting for him to tell me about the conversation, and he knows it. Jeremy steps away from me, and my hair whips in front of me, so that I can't see Jeremy's face anymore. I realize he'd been blocking the wind for me.

"He didn't tell me anything," he says, and it's strange not to be able to see him when he's talking to me. I press my hair behind my ears. "Nothing that matters," Jeremy says with finality, as though that's that and there's no point in talking anymore.

"It matters to me. You promised," I insist. I sound like a spoiled five-year-old.

"Jesus, Sternin, he didn't tell me anything. I'm sorry." Jeremy's voiced is raised. He doesn't sound sorry.

"You don't sound sorry."

"Well, fuck it, Sternin"—he throws his hands in the air helplessly—"I'm dealing with some shit of my own here."

"God, you didn't even try, did you? You didn't even try to talk to him about my dad. Did you even mention it to him at all?" My toes curl and clench inside my shoes.

"I told you, Sternin—what, you think I'm a liar now?"

"I don't know what to think. You promised to help me and

now you're yelling at me like I made you do it. It was your fuck-ing idea."

"I tried. Jesus!" Jeremy is shouting now. "What the hell is the matter with you? You think your father dying over a decade ago matters anywhere near as much as my sister dying now?"

"Yes, I think it's important," I say, almost yelling. "I thought you did too."

I can't believe I said that. I can't believe I'm being so selfish. I should be focused on Kate. I should remember that we can talk about my father some other time, sometime later; tomorrow, even. But I can't; I'm too mad. I only confided in Jeremy because I thought he understood that it was important; I thought he under-stood me. But maybe he never did.

He's back up on his throne now, a million miles away from me. My problems aren't nearly as important as those of the royal fam-ily. Even if they're not all that different.

I'm seething. I can't remember having ever been this mad at someone. I only realize I'm crying because when the wind blows, my tears are cold against my face.

Quietly, like it's the beginning of an apology, Jeremy says, "Look, Sternin," but I cut him off.

"Fuck you, Jeremy." My anger has made me feel strong. "I trusted you. Fuck you." I turn away from him and stomp into my lobby and press for the elevator. I don't turn around in case he's still there, watching me as I wait like an idiot for the elevator to come. It's taking forever. Of all the times for it not to be here. So much for a dramatic exit. I'm angry at the elevator now too. These things don't happen to people who live in the suburbs.

But when it finally comes, I step inside and turn around, and as the door closes, I see that he's not there anyway, not waiting to say anything more, and I'm sure he walked away just as soon as I turned my back to him.

Later, when I can't sleep, I look again at the picture of my parents. I turn the light on this time, stare at my mother's legs across my father's lap, his hand supporting her back. I want the picture to tell me something; to reveal something about the man my father was, the life he and my mother had. But I've stared at it before; the picture has nothing else to tell me. I resist the urge to crumple it up before putting it back in its place between the pages of the book.

❋ ❋ ❋

Jeremy isn't in school on Thursday, which is also the last day before winter break begins. School will be out until the new year. I'm not surprised, since he said he was getting tested today. In the light of day, I can see that I should call him, see how it went, see if it hurt as much as he was scared it would. I consider leaving physics class—pretending to go to the bathroom and calling him. I go so far as to begin to scoot off the tall lab stool. The tips of my shoes hit the floor, but then I change my mind. I slide back onto my seat and stare straight ahead at the chalkboard. I can't forget that Jeremy and I fought. I know I said awful things, and I can't imagine he'd want to hear from me right now.

But I want to know that Jeremy's okay; that Kate's okay. I tell myself that if something serious had happened, Jeremy would still call me.

School is different without Jeremy here. Lonelier. I eat lunch in the library. Over the last few weeks, Jeremy and I worked through lunch all the time. Sat in the library going over SAT words, taking bites of sandwiches in between. I never felt lonely then. But now I can't imagine how I ever sat here by myself.

I wonder if Jeremy will come over for his bedtime cigarette. I wonder if his parents will ask why I'm not coming over for dinner tonight. It's not fair that Jeremy doesn't have to be lonely without me; he has his family to eat with tonight and I'll be eating alone in front of the TV. And when he comes back to school, he'll still have plenty of people to sit with at lunchtime.

17

My mother doesn't comment when I walk in the door at three-fifteen on the nose, but I'm sure she notices it. I haven't come straight home after school in ages, or if I have, Jeremy is with me and it's only to pick up some things before heading down to the Coles'. Even yesterday, Jeremy and I went to get some coffee after school before he went home for dinner with Dr. Kleinbaum. I know my mother is dying to ask why I'm home so early. I bet she thinks it's something tragic, like something terrible happened to Kate, and I bet she's so excited at the idea that I would know before the rest of the city because she thinks that as far as the Coles are concerned, I'm practically family.

Then I walk past her on the way to my room—she's sitting on the living room couch, reading some book I know she stole off my shelves. No, I feel guilty for thinking something like that. However much my mother loves her New York City gossip, however much she'd like to be a part of the Coles' world, she's been through tragedy herself (even if I don't know the damn details), and I'm sure she'd never derive pleasure from being the first to know something awful like that. No matter how hot the gossip. She chews the pinkie finger on her left hand when she reads, just like the sixth graders do when you see them sitting in the hallway between classes, backs up against the lockers, eyes scanning the chapter they're behind on in *Little Women*.

❈ ❈ ❈

It's six-fifteen when my mother knocks on my door. I'm studying, even though today was the last day of school before winter break. I was hoping that physics would keep my mind from wandering and landing on Jeremy and Kate.

My mom opens the door. "Honey, are you staying home for dinner?"

I pretend to be completely absorbed in my work. My back is to her because I'm lying on my stomach, my books splayed out across the bed in front of me. I arch my back and turn my neck to face her. I'm scared she'll ask why I'm not at the Coles'.

"Honey?"

"Hmm?"

"Are you going to be home for dinner?"

"Oh, yeah, I guess." I try to sound like I haven't thought about it. "I'm not really that hungry," I lie.

"Well, I was going to order something, if you'd like that. I wasn't expecting that you'd be home." She says that as though it explains her not having cooked.

"Sure. Whatever you want."

"Oh, I don't know." She steps into the room; sits on the edge of my bed, disturbing my notes. It occurs to me that this is the first time we'll have had dinner together since that night at the diner. I remember how sad I made her that night, how her voice dropped when I brought up my father, and I consider telling her that I have to study, so that I can eat in my room and not have to sit across the table from her.

"Maybe Chinese?" she suggests.

"Sure, that's fine."

"Or we could order from that diner you like."

"Okay." I keep my eyes on my physics text.

"Or pizza—how about pizza?"

I put down my highlighter and look up.

"Mom, really, whatever you want is fine with me. I just have a lot of work to get done tonight."

"Oh," she says, and for just a second, I think she looks heartbreakingly, achingly sad. The expression leaves her face almost before I think I see it. I wonder if she misses me. Sometimes, even though we're both right here in this apartment, I miss her.

"I'm sorry, Mom. It's just . . . physics."

"Jeremy isn't tutoring you anymore?"

"No, he is." I swing around so that I'm sitting up, cross-legged on the bed, facing her. "He was just home sick today, so, you know, he can't help me." I look her straight in the eye when I lie. She knows nothing about my friendship with him, I think, so she can't tell that I'm lying. Technically, I don't even have to be studying now. I wonder if my mother remembers that school is out for the next week and a half.

"Oh, that's too bad. I hope he feels better soon."

"Yeah, me too," I say, like it's no big deal. "Anyway, pizza sounds good. Pepperoni and onions on my half, okay?"

"Okay." She gets up from the bed and heads for the door. I lie back down to face my notes, so that my back is to the door again.

"What's the matter?" she says.

"Huh?" I say, frightened, swinging back around to face her, messing up my notes even more. I don't want to tell her what's the matter with me tonight.

"With Jeremy? What kind of sick is he?" Oh. My shoulders slump with relief; I'd already forgotten about that lie.

I shrug. "Some kind of flu that's been going around."

"Oh, I've heard about that."

I stifle a mean laugh. Since I made up that a flu was going around, I'm either benefiting from the coincidence that there is an actual flu going around, or from my mother's desire to act like she's in the know.

"I hope that he's staying away from Kate," she says. "I mean, with all that chemo, her immune system must be compromised."

"Yeah." I hadn't thought about that. "I'm sure he is." By this time, my mother has heard the details of Kate's illness through the grapevine. I get a little guilty satisfaction from knowing that I know so much more than she does, and that I know because the Coles have told me themselves. After all, she's kept so much from me.

"Of course. He'd never jeopardize her health."

"Of course."

She pauses at my door. I wonder what more she wants. But then she turns and I hear her padding down the hall, and then ordering the pizza. When it comes, I do drag myself out of my room and sit at the table, but I bring my physics book with me. I just kind of stare at it while I eat.

"You can have the last slice, honey."

"That's okay, I'm full."

"Me too," my mother says, and laughs. I don't really under-stand why both of us being full is funny, but I smile back. And I def-initely don't know why I choose to ruin this moment by asking, "Do I look like my father?"

"What?" she says, anxiety making her voice high-pitched, turn-ing the end of her laughter into cackles.

"Well, it's just, I look nothing like you—I figure I must take after him."

She doesn't say anything, and I keep going. Maybe I'm testing her strength, or maybe I'm testing mine. Certainly I'm justifying her fear of being alone with me.

I lean back in my chair, cross my legs under me. "I'm taller than you, and I have straight hair, and my eyes are gray and yours are green. Plus, my mouth is much wider than yours." I list all this as though she needs to be told. As though it's not evident to any-one who sees us just walking down the street. Strangers would as-sume I take after my father.

"You've seen pictures of him," she says slowly, maybe angrily. "Judge for yourself."

"I guess I meant, do you think I look like him? Do I remind you of him?"

She doesn't say anything and begins to gather our plates, forks, and knives. I follow her into the kitchen.

"Can't you at least tell me that?" I say.

"No," she says, and I think she's refusing me, but then she goes on. "You don't remind me of him. You didn't ever—you never got to spend time with him, and so you never picked up his mannerisms, the way he gestured when he talked, the odd expressions he used—things like that."

She continues, "Maybe you picked up some of his habits from me—I mean, I'm sure I picked things like that up from him, living with him for all those years. But by the time . . . by the end, I couldn't remember which ones had started out as his and which as mine."

She stops loading the dishwasher long enough to remember one thing. "He used the word 'ma'am' a lot, I think as a joke. He'd say 'Yes, ma'am' to me when I was giving him a hard time. I started saying 'ma'am' too, to my mother, to friends; I just randomly picked up the word. I don't remember when I stopped using it."

The dishes are all in the dishwasher, and she wipes her hands on the dish towel by the sink.

"Anyway"—she looks at the table, at my physics book—"good luck with your studying." I take the cue and head back to my room. It's the most I can remember her ever telling me about my father.

I think: I'll tell Jeremy when he comes over for his bedtime cigarette. And then I remember that he isn't coming. And then all I can think about is Jeremy. I want to know how Kate is, and I want to know how Jeremy's test went today. I take forever to fall asleep that night. I pile three blankets on top of me, thinking that their weight will help keep me still. For the first time in a while, I imagine my fairy godmother is there—but even she can't comfort me.

❈ ❈ ❈

I don't hear from Jeremy during winter break. My mother and I spend the holidays as we always do: pretty much exactly the same way we spend the rest of the year, but with more free time. On Christmas Day, we always go to the movies, come home, and order in Chinese food. This year, we go to see the new Woody Allen movie and it's sold out when we get there, so we have to wait for the next showing.

"So this is where all the Jews are," I joke to my mother, who laughs for a long time.

The movie theater is across the street from the ice cream parlor where Jeremy, Kate, and I went. Maybe Kate is doing better now; maybe she's gotten the bone marrow and it's working. I picture them eating ice cream; I don't think I've ever wished so hard for one of my fantasies to come true.

I spend New Year's Eve fighting with computer customer service, since I can't access my e-mail. I don't know why I'm so determined to check it anyway. Maybe I think that there will be a "Happy New Year" e-mail from Jeremy, or from Kate. I tell myself that if only I can get online, I will e-mail them, find out how Kate is, wish them happy holidays. But I know it won't come true. I'm too scared; I don't think Jeremy would want to hear from me right now.

But it feels strange not to know where Jeremy is. Maybe he's at the hospital, recovering from donating bone marrow—although I don't even know how long you have to stay at the hospital for something like that. For all I know, he's only a couple dozen blocks south of me, in their den, watching the ball drop with Kate asleep on his shoulder. I'm already in bed. I feel left out.

❋ ❋ ❋

Jeremy isn't at school the first day back. No one ever does this— takes off the last day before the break and the first day after—the school doesn't like kids' families trying to extend vacation, so it's an unexcused absence and you get detention. I'm near tears in physics class. Maybe it's because I don't understand anything, even though I studied hard over the break, and without Jeremy there to help me, it seems like I never will. A row of F's and D's stretches out frighteningly in front of me. Or maybe it's because physics was almost fun with Jeremy here—school was more fun—and having lost my best friend, I hardly know what to do with myself.

I decide to allow myself to fantasize about something; anything to distract me from the teacher, whose words I can't follow, and from the way that Jeremy's empty stool behind me feels like it's staring at me. I rest my chin in my hand. I hope the teacher doesn't notice I've stopped taking notes.

I imagine that Jeremy sprints into class, getting away with being late as only he can. Everyone stops what they're doing. Everybody stares at Jeremy—the big grin on his face, the happiness he seems to have brought with him into the room. He comes straight toward me and scoops me up into a hug—a dramatic gesture he would never make in real life.

"Kate's going to be okay," he whispers into my hair. The bone marrow worked. Kate is well. Everything will be fine and Jeremy isn't mad at me anymore—he's too happy to be bothered about our stupid fight. He didn't call because he was at the hospital so much, taking care of her, recovering from donating the marrow. Kate is well, and she can eat sundaes again, and she'll come back to school and her hair will grow long and she'll cheer for Jeremy when his name is called at graduation. Just like I knew she would.

Then the classroom door opens—not in my fantasy, in real life.

I actually spin around on my seat, just in case it really is Jeremy. But it's not: it's the assistant principal, and she's calling my name.

"Connelly?"

Everyone turns from the chalkboard to the door at the back of the room, where the assistant principal is standing timidly. Then everyone turns to look at me. I think I'm still looking for Jeremy.

"Please come with me."

I gather up my books and grab my bag. I must be in trouble, but I can't think of what I've done to get the assistant principal to call me out of class. I avoid everyone's faces—I wonder what reasons they're coming up with for my being called away. I hate the way it feels, having everyone looking at me. I wish I'd dressed better; I wish my bag wasn't full to overflowing, my ponytail was a little neater.

"There's a phone call for you," she says once the door to the science lab has closed behind me. Quietly, like she doesn't want anyone to hear.

"A phone call?" Only something urgent could make them come get me like this. "Oh God, what's wrong? Has my mother—"

"It's not your mother." I follow her to her office. I wonder why she's being so quiet, but it occurs to me that it's because any of the kids or faculty in the halls might hear and she doesn't want them to. I still don't think that it's Jeremy; I still don't think that it's because anything has happened to Kate. My fantasy has made me believe that maybe Kate can and will be well again.

I pick up the phone and hold it gently to my ear, barely touching me.

"Hello?"

"Sternin?"

"Jer?" It's a relief just to say his name. "Jeremy." I've missed it so much that I say it again.

"I'm sorry to get you out of physics."

"It's okay," I say. "Of course it's okay." And then I know why he's calling, why his call was enough to get me out of physics. It's why, for the rest of my life, I'll wish I'd called to wish them happy holidays, or a happy new year, or called just to say hi. And it's why we've skipped over the making-up part of our fight. Best friends can do that, I guess.

I hear Jeremy take a deep breath, and then he says, "Kate's died."

I don't say anything. I stare at the carpet on the floor of the assistant principal's office, a hideous shade of maroon that makes her whole office seem dark and weighty. I hear Jeremy's voice in my head again: *Kate's died*. There's a catch in it, something I've never heard before. It's like he said it but he still can't believe it. I wonder how many times he's had to say it since it happened, how many family members and friends he's already called. I wonder if every time he says it, he believes it a little more.

"Sternin?" he prompts.

"I'm sorry, Jeremy," I say, half apologizing for her death, half apologizing for my silence.

Then I say, "I can come down there. I can leave right now."

"Not right now. It's strange here."

Maybe he's still angry at me. Maybe he's angrier still because I didn't call. I bite my lip.

"But I'll see you later tonight," he says, and I know he means he'll come over for a cigarette. Then he hangs up, so I do too.

The assistant principal is watching me like she's waiting for me to tell her something. I remember Jeremy's voice saying, "Kate's died." It's not as though I'd forgotten it, but while I was on the phone, I couldn't really think about the way that it sounded. I'd been trying to say the right thing, waiting to hear what Jeremy was going to say next. Now I close my eyes, and I hear Jeremy saying it again: *Kate's died.*

I sit down in the desk chair and cry. I cry so long that the assistant principal calls my mother to come pick me up. I cry so much that I'm sure my tears are making a wet spot on the ugly carpet, so much that none of the tissues the assistant principal hands me make a bit of difference. I feel pieces of them sticking to my face. I'm crying for Kate, and I'm crying for the Coles, and I'm crying for Jeremy and me, and for how happy I am to have him back, and how distraught I am that this is the reason why.

And maybe I'm crying for my dad; maybe I'm mourning him too.

18

My mother is white when she picks me up. As soon as I see her, I realize that the whole time I'd been crying, I'd been thinking, Oh God, I want my mother.

The assistant principal must have told her about Kate, but I don't believe that my mother can understand what this means to me. She looks like she wants to hold me but she doesn't know how. I wish, more than anything, that I could just climb into her lap and be rocked from side to side—but I'm too big for that, and anyway, I don't know how.

My mother walks me to my locker so I can get my books (it's inconceivable that I wouldn't take my homework with me), and when we step outside, my eyes are dry and my face is clean because I stopped to rinse it with cold water. She hasn't said much—hasn't said anything except for "Hello" to the assistant principal and "Is that all your books?" to me.

I wonder what it was like the first time I saw her after my father died. I wonder if she was this quiet. I don't remember how I found out that he had died—whether she was the one who told me. We walk home quickly, both of us wearing boots that click on the cement. It's freezing out and the air is cold in my nose, down into my lungs, and out again in smoke before my face. We pass a flower shop. I turn to face my mother. "I want to stop—I could order some flowers to send to the Coles."

"No, sweetie, don't send flowers."

"Why not?" I say meanly. "They're my friends, even if they never invited you anywhere."

My mother looks hurt—I only said that because I understand what an invitation from the Coles would have meant to her. Still, she's patient with me.

"No, honey. Jews just don't send flowers."

"Why not?"

"Umm," she says, looking up, over my head, "I don't know. It's the kind of thing you just find out."

"When?" I ask.

She doesn't say anything. We walk in silence; now we're only a block from home. In my head, I am repeating a line: *Among the dead, there are so many thousands of the beautiful.* I can hear it being said. I can't remember what it's from; can't recognize whose voice is saying it. I'm sure it's from a book; maybe it was a teacher, saying it in class. The line stays in my head for days, and it will be a long time before I figure out where it's from.

Among the dead, there are so many thousands of the beautiful. My father is one. And now Kate is one too. Maybe my father will take care of Kate. And then I realize something I never thought of: I don't know if my father was—or would have been—a good father. I don't know if he's someone I want to watch Kate. I am filled with a need to do something, anything, for Kate.

We're standing across from our apartment house, waiting for

the light to change so we can cross the street. My mother looks at my hands: my fingers are cold, and I'm not wearing gloves, and I realize that I left them in the bathroom when I went to rinse my face off. I stuff my hands in my pockets. I ask my mother, "Well, what can I do, or send?"

"We'll order some food when we get home. Or sometimes they'll ask for donations to a charity."

"But how will I know? How will I find out what charity?"

"It'll be in the obituary," she says, and begins to walk again.

"But then how do they know that I sent it?" It sounds like I want credit. It's not that; I just want to do the right thing, whatever it is you're supposed to do when this happens, and I have no idea what that is.

But my mother does. My mother knows that Jews don't send flowers and she knows that they will probably ask for a donation instead and she will know exactly what words I should say when I see them at the funeral, the words to put in the condolence card I will send. (And she knows about condolence cards too, the existence of which never occurred to me.) My mother knows all of this. She knows it from experience.

❀ ❀ ❀

It's after midnight and I'm waiting for Jeremy. I didn't stay up this late on New Year's. I'm not impatient. I know he'll come. I'm looking, again, at the picture of my parents. My mother is asleep at the other end of the apartment but I'm scared she'll wake, come in to check on me, see me looking at the picture. I shut my door and sit down against it so that I'm leaning on it, holding it closed.

I wonder why I was so drawn to this picture. There were

pictures from their wedding day, pictures with me in them, pictures with my grandparents. Why does this picture mean so much to me?

And then I see it: something I never noticed before. I recognize the chair that they're sitting on. I recognize it from the house we lived in before my father died. I even remember that the cloth that covered it was itchy. I wonder what happened to the chair when we moved here. I want to ask my mother, but I won't. I can't. I can't even tell her that I have the photograph.

I'm putting the picture away when my phone rings.

"I'm downstairs."

"I'll be right there."

He's already finishing a cigarette when I get downstairs. When I hug him, it smells like he hasn't stopped smoking all day today. Once, he made a joke that it was ironic that Kate's illness made him smoke more, rather than discourage him as one might think. "You know," he added when I looked at him blankly. "The whole cancer connection." At the time, we'd both laughed. It shouldn't have been funny, so our laughter was guilt-ridden.

"I'm glad to see you," I say.

"Me too," he says.

"Do you want to—"

"No. I don't. Let's just not talk about it yet."

"That's fine too."

Jeremy lights two cigarettes, passes one to me. A few weeks ago, he got us both fingerless gloves, just for smoking, and we're both wearing them now.

"Jeremy." I say his name slowly, and I wait until he is looking at me to continue.

"I shouldn't have not called." I don't know why I say it like that, so I say it again, better this time: "I mean, I should have called."

Jeremy nods.

"I'm so sorry."

Jeremy drops his cigarette on the ground and crushes it. He looks up, blinking. I wonder if he is trying not to cry. I am.

"Let's not worry about that now," Jeremy says finally. "I don't want to worry about that right now. I just want to be here. Okay?"

I nod. "Okay."

Jeremy lights another cigarette. "The funeral's so quick," he says, exhaling.

"I know. It's a Jewish thing. My mother told me."

"She never struck me as particularly religious."

"She's not. But I think her parents were."

"So she'd know, then."

"Yeah, she'd know."

Jeremy looks up as he takes a drag from his cigarette. "I didn't know," he exhales.

I nod. "I guess you only really find out when it happens to you."

"Unless you're religious."

"Right." I pause. "Did you know Jews don't send flowers?"

He shrugs. "No one told my parents' friends that. The house reeks of lilies. We were going to run something in the paper about 'In lieu of flowers, send a donation to the American Cancer Society,' but we weren't fast enough."

"Guess not."

"You know, until, like, this morning, I always thought that 'in lieu of' meant almost the exact opposite of 'instead of.' I thought it meant . . . I don't know, like, '*By way of* flowers, please send them to the American Cancer Society.' Like, 'Send flowers there for their sick people, 'cause our sick person is gone, so send them to people who can still appreciate it.' "

I laugh unexpectedly. "Oh my God, so did I! Once my grandmother was having a party and I asked her what she was having in lieu of food!"

"Liar."

"I swear to God. She laughed at me and told me what it really meant."

Jeremy grins wide, and then the grin fades into one of his crooked smiles.

"I've been Kate's big brother for as long as I can remember—I was only four when she was born, even though I always felt so much older than she was." He takes a sharp breath in and exhales slowly, and I wait for him to go on. "And now I'm not a big brother anymore. And, I don't know, I guess that was always the first thing I thought of myself as being."

I want to tell Jeremy that he's my big brother, even if it's not the same thing. That even though we're the same age, I look up to him and he seems years older, wiser, and more worldly than I'll ever be. But I know it's not the same, so I keep quiet—except for my sniffling, which I pretend is only because of the cold and has nothing to do with the tears hanging on to the edge of my eyelashes.

"It's good to be here," Jeremy says, and he puts his arm around me and we stand like that, in the cold, for a long time. I know I'm crying and I suspect he is too, but I don't look up at him to see. The next day, I won't even remember his leaving or my coming back up on the elevator and getting into bed. No, the last memory I have of that evening is of standing close to Jeremy in the cold, watching his breath come out in puffs of smoke.

19

I want very much to wear the right thing to the funeral: it feels like it is the last thing I will ever get to do for Kate, and I must do it perfectly. I think wearing all black would be presumptuous of me; that should be reserved for family members. I will wear gray or navy, and only a little black. I don't even know whether this is my first funeral. I imagine my two-year-old self at my father's funeral, sitting on some willing grandparent's lap, sucking my thumb—something that would normally be forbidden, but surely no one would have said no to me that day—and watching the service, not understanding what it all meant. I see myself hot, cranky, and hungry; I imagine my hair being stroked; strangers kissing me, pitying my mother and me.

It's easier to think I didn't go, and so I imagine the adults saying, She's too young. Leave her home with the sitter—a funeral's no place for a child.

My mother and I take a cab together to the funeral home, even though it's only eight blocks away. There's a crowd outside, people waiting to get in. My mother had insisted we leave early. I thought she was just nervous about being late. But maybe she knew you get there early so you can see the family first, crowd into a little room and express your condolences, before taking your seats. Maybe she knew that afterward, when the family members rush into the black cars that take them to the cemetery, there might not be time.

I didn't ask my mother to come with me today; I knew she would come. The room next to the chapel is packed. Jeremy is surrounded, and I don't think I should squeeze past all these people to see him. I saw him last night, and I'm sure I'll see him again tonight. So my mother and I stand in the corner, waiting for it to be time to move into the chapel, to sit and watch. I'm surprised when Jeremy is suddenly standing next to me. He leans down quickly, whispers in my ear, "Go and hug my mother. She loves you." His breath is warm on my neck. And then he's gone, back in that crowd of people.

I don't know why Jeremy's asked me to go hug his mother. She's probably surrounded by her family and her closest friends. I'll be intruding. But I also don't want to let Jeremy down; he said she loved me. I know Jeremy wouldn't have said it if it wasn't true, but I barely know her. I don't know why she would particularly care about seeing me now.

Kate would know, I think. If I asked Kate, she'd be able to explain it to me.

I start to look for Mrs. Cole. My mother follows me through the crowd and then I see her, Mrs. Cole, sitting on a velvety couch, silently staring ahead of her. People are talking to her, or anyway, talking to each other around her, keeping their hands on her shoulder, her knee, over her hands folded in her lap. I walk straight toward her. My mother hangs back; I'm relieved that she understands not to follow me. Mrs. Cole's face almost brightens when she sees me; her arms extend toward me like she knew I was coming to hug her. She rocks me back and forth, or I rock her. When I let go, she takes my hands and squeezes them, and I know that she knows how sorry I am, how much I loved Kate, and how much I love her son. And I know that's what Jeremy was talking about when he said that she loves me.

I turn around, see my mother waiting. A flicker of something I don't recognize passes across her face—is it jealousy? Not jealousy that I'm so close with the Coles, but jealousy of the way Mrs. Cole and I just held each other.

We file into the chapel, and soon I am watching Jeremy: first the back of his head as he sits in the front row—his brown hair that's almost wavy, but not quite—and then his face when he gets up to speak. Neither of his parents speaks. He is wearing a dark gray suit and it occurs to me that I've never seen him dressed so nicely and that he looks very handsome and tall, speaking about his sister without crying like the rest of us. The only thing that gives him away is the way that he's digging his hands into the side of the podium, hanging on like it's holding him up—but I think you'd have to look very closely to see that. Otherwise, he looks collected. He looks regal. I realize this is where princes earn their titles: their titles are something they must live up to, and Jeremy is doing that now at this Upper East Side funeral—he is keeping everything together and being every bit the man that we all need him to be. And it's strange, and maybe a little condescending of me, but I feel enormously, tenderly, and warmly proud of him.

I wonder what it's like to be strong like Jeremy. As I sit in the pew, my body curls up around itself, like it's trying to keep me warm. My shoulders are hunched and I'm slouching as low as I can, my arms crossed in front of me, my hands clutching opposite elbows, like I think I will fall apart if I let go.

But my mother is sitting up straight next to me. She is staring straight ahead, focused intently on the back of the head of the man sitting in front of her. I look up at Jeremy, and I see that he is doing the same thing: staring straight in front of him at the back of the room. Neither he nor my mother flinches, whatever words he says. They just hold their gaze in front of them as tightly as I'm holding my arms. Maybe they aren't so different.

Kate is in a plain, closed wooden casket at the front of the room. The only thing that gives anything away about the person inside it is its size. It's short, so you can guess that it's a young person. Before the service began, people were walking up to the casket and touching it like they were saying goodbye.

I didn't go near the casket. I don't see how touching a piece of wood will make it any easier to say goodbye to Kate. But it feels a little better now, listening to Jeremy talking about his sister.

"I don't know how to tell you about Kate. I don't know what words are the right ones to use so that you know that she was more than funny, or smart, or beautiful, or kind. But I can tell you this: Kate would know the right words. A friend of ours once told me that Kate always knew the right things to say."

Startled, I drop my soaked tissue into my lap and sit up a little straighter. Because that was me: I was the friend who said that. I look around—no one can tell, of course, that he was talking about me. And even though I'm still crying, it's somehow comforting to think that this is something that only Jeremy, Kate, and I know.

When I look down at my lap, I see that a fresh tissue has

replaced the one I dropped. My mother is stuffing the dirty one into her purse.

"Thank you," I whisper, and she nods at me, almost smiling.

When the service is over, the family files out in a different direction from everyone else, to what I guess is a room beside the chapel where they can get ready for the trip to the cemetery. A crowd gathers outside on the sidewalk, everyone waiting to say goodbye to the Coles. It's remarkably cold today. There are a bunch of students here; some teachers too. I wonder if the students are getting excused absences and I wonder who's covering the teachers' classes. I wonder if they made an announcement. I bet they'll hold a special assembly to help everyone deal with the loss—an hour I know Jeremy will spend hiding out somewhere else.

I button my coat up to my chin; dig my hat out of my bag and put it on. My mother pulls on thin leather gloves that I can't imagine will keep her hands very warm. Someone grabs me from behind. It's Jeremy, and he drags me around the corner.

"I want to have a cigarette before we leave, but I can't do it in front of everyone," he says, talking fast. I nod; everyone is out here, and they'd be mobbing him.

I look back for my mother—I don't know if she saw Jeremy grab me. She might be looking for me. Jeremy takes me to the driveway behind the funeral home. There is a hearse parked next to where we stand. While Jeremy smokes, Kate's casket is brought out and loaded into it. People who work here do it, like professional pallbearers. Jeremy acts like he doesn't see, so I do too.

My eyes sting in the cold air from crying so much earlier, and smoke clouds Jeremy's face.

"You did really well in there," I say. "I was really proud of you."

"Thanks, Connie," he says, and lights a second cigarette. He seems to be in no hurry. I wonder if his parents are waiting, if he told them he needed a few minutes.

"You have to do something for me," he says.

I look up at him, thinking, Anything. I'll do anything you need me to. But I just say, "What?"

He inhales deeply. "I was thinking about you almost as soon as Kate died, thinking about how she'd died and the way it ended, thinking about how I was there and then the doctor explained every detail of what it was that killed her, why it had happened at that moment." He pauses, and then he says, "It meant something to me, hearing all that."

I picture Jeremy standing in a hospital hallway, a doctor talking to him, trying to make Kate's death make sense.

"Connelly, you have to know. You're sixteen years old and something happened when you were a baby that you couldn't have understood, but you're old enough now. Your mother botched it up, and now you have to demand that she do it better."

"I have to demand that she do it better?"

"Yes." He nods, and I can tell that he's given this some thought, that he came up with the phrase "demand that she do it better" some time before and has been waiting to say it to me.

"You have to tell her that she was wrong to keep you in the dark this long and you can forgive her now, but she has to tell you the truth."

"I don't understand."

Jeremy looks down at me, not impatiently, but maybe he's

wondering why it's taking me so long to figure out what he means. "Ask your mother. Just ask her. All this figuring it out, trying to find out—it's bullshit. It's *beside* the point. You should find out from your mother, not because I got some doctor to break his confidence. It's your business, Connelly; it's your history, and it's time for your mother to tell you. So ask her."

"Ask her what?" I say, truly confused.

"Connelly, are you listening to me?" Jeremy tosses away his cigarette, puts his hands on my shoulders, and looks right at me, and hard. "You have to go home right now and ask your mother how your father died. I can't imagine how lost I would feel if all I knew was that Kate had died and I didn't know what it was that killed her. Can you imagine? Just being told that my sister died without any kind of explanation?" Jeremy's voice catches for a second. He takes a breath and continues, "Cancer, car accident, whatever it was, it's making you who you are, so you need to know what it is. It matters, Connelly. Maybe it shouldn't, but it does. It gives sense to it."

"I can't ask her," I say, and twist out of his hands. The lump that's been in my throat since Kate died begins to rise.

"Why?"

I shake my head. "I can't. You don't understand."

"Explain it to me."

"I can't, I can't." I heave the words with my breath. The lump in my throat hurts so much, I can't catch my breath. I begin to cry, and I really didn't think I could cry any more today.

Jeremy takes my hand. "Explain it to me."

I don't know what to say. It seems wrong that he should be

comforting me. But I understand: even though my father died years ago, I am only beginning to mourn him now, just like Jeremy is only beginning to mourn Kate. And Jeremy knows that, even if I didn't.

"Explain it to me," he repeats.

"It would hurt her. You don't know. I can't do that to her."

"Connelly, you have to."

"You don't know." My face is soaking wet again. "I asked her once, just once, and nothing has ever been the same. I've never been able to just—I don't know—get into her bed and watch TV. She couldn't even hug me after Kate died."

"Maybe you need to just get this out of the way, then, Connelly. Maybe then you can even have your mother back."

"It's been too long. I can't. Questions—questions like that are too much. They ruin everything."

"No they don't. It's the exact opposite."

I shake my head. I can't. He can't make me.

"You can do it, Connelly," he says, like he knows what I'm thinking. "You can and you have to."

I don't say anything. He sounds so positive that he's right.

"You'll feel better." With his heel, he grinds the cigarette he'd tossed away and then he puts his arms around me. "You'll feel better," he repeats into my hair, and he kisses the top of my head.

"I gotta go," he says. "My parents are waiting."

"Okay." I'm distracted now, thinking about my mother, about what I have to ask her now. Then I realize I should be thinking about him, at least somewhat. "Call me if you need anything. And give your family my love, and—"

"I know. You too."

Jeremy smiles and heads inside through the back entrance, and I walk back out to the front to find my mother.

"Come on, let's go," I say.

"You don't want to wait to see the Coles again?"

"Another time. We'll go to shiva tomorrow or something." "Shiva" is a new word to me, another thing my mother taught me. I knew that it meant prayers for the dead, but I never knew it meant visiting someone's home, eating catered bagels, sitting on the couch and keeping the mourners company.

She doesn't argue, and together we walk home.

20

At home, I experience a phenomenon that someday, years later, when I have been to more funerals and have experienced it after every single one, I will call the post-funeral jitters: when almost anything can make you explode into a fit of giggles because you've been holding in all this nervousness—you've literally just cried yourself silly. Honestly, I have no idea if anyone else experiences the post-funeral jitters, but when we walk in the door, my mother asks me what I want to eat and I think she's said that the funeral was neat and we can't stop laughing. The thing that finally makes me stop is the thought that maybe she broke down giggling after my father's funeral. And I think that the thing that makes her stop is when she realizes that I'm not laughing anymore.

We've just walked in the door; we'd been hanging our coats in the hall closet when she'd asked. She closes the closet door and turns back to me.

"Honey, I'm so sorry."

"I know," I say, and then I walk into the living room. I'm scared. She thinks I'm acting strangely because of Kate. She doesn't know what I'm about to do. I think I should work up to it somehow, use Kate as a segue. But I don't want to use Kate like that, and subtlety has gotten me nowhere so far.

I turn around to face her, and then I say, "Mom, how did my dad die?"

She doesn't say anything. She sits at the table and I sit across the room, on the sofa. She takes off her shoes and turns in her chair to face me.

"What?"

I repeat the plain question: "How did my dad die?"

"Your father died when you were two."

"I know." That's not the answer to my question. "And I was too young to remember much of anything about it or anything about him."

My mom sighs. Maybe she thinks that it's only Kate's death that has brought this on; maybe she thinks she can still avoid telling me. "What do you want to know?"

My hands are still cold, so I sit on them to warm them. I speak slowly and softly. "Mom, please. How did my dad die?" It's the third time I've said it. Every time, it's gotten a little easier, like learning a new language.

"You were too young to know."

"I'm older now."

"No. You were too young."

"Mom, look at me, please. We're not talking about when it happened; that was fourteen years ago. It's been fourteen years. You can tell me now." I pause. She is looking at her feet, resting them on top of the shoes she just took off. "You have to tell me now," I say.

"He was sick," she says.

"I know; he had cancer."

She looks up at me, surprised. "I didn't know you knew that."

I know she wants me to explain how I knew; I know she's racking her mind for the ways I might have found out, planning angry phone calls to my grandparents. But I know I have to keep her focused or I will lose this chance.

"But it wasn't the cancer that killed him, right?"

"He was sick," she says again.

"How sick?"

"Very sick," she almost whispers.

"Not just the cancer?"

"No," she says, staring past me to the window behind me. "Not just the cancer. They thought he would survive the cancer."

"It was leukemia?"

"Yes. But not like Kate's. His prognosis was good." This surprises me. Jeremy had said they had the same kind of cancer.

"What else was he sick with?"

She pauses, and I think she's going to cry. "Please, Connelly, it doesn't matter now. It's been years."

"It matters to me."

"Oh God, sweetie, please." She puts her head in her hands, presses hard on her temples.

My hands are falling asleep beneath me, but I don't move. "Please just tell me. Just . . . just get it over with." I stand up and walk close to her, and take her hand. "I'll help—he was sick, right? He got sick after the cancer?"

"No," she says, staring at my hand holding hers. "He had been sick before the cancer. When they began treatment—chemo—he went off his other medicine."

"And that's what killed him?"

"Yes," she says, and I can tell she thinks we're through. She drops my hand and leans down to pick her shoes up from the floor, stands to go into her bedroom. She's going to put her shoes away, take off her funeral suit, and change her clothes, just like I will. But not until we're done.

"What was it?"

She turns and looks at me. "Honey, it's been a long day. For both of us." I can hear the desperation in her voice. Her shoes are clutched in her right hand. She is, in her way, begging me to stop. "Let's rest. I'll get us some food and we'll relax and tomorrow we'll go to the Coles'. This has been a hard day for you."

I walk to where she's standing. "Mommy, listen to me. You have to tell me. It's mine to know. It's what I'm made out of." I can't remember the last time I called her Mommy.

"No," she says emphatically. "It is not what you're made out of." She drops her shoes to the floor with a bang and takes hold of my left arm. "It is not what you're made out of. You were too young to understand. It hasn't left a mark on you."

"Hasn't left a mark on me?" I say, almost shouting. "Mom, I grew up without a dad. Of course that left a mark on me!"

"Then why does it matter how he died? All that matters is that he's dead."

"What did he do, Mom? There's something you don't want me to know, something you think you can't tell me. But you can, and you have to. And I can take it—I promise. What I can't take is not knowing." I twist my arm from her grasp and hold her hand instead, gently. "Mommy, please. Please."

"He was sick," she whispers, not looking at me.

"How?"

"Very sick. He'd always been sick, but he managed it. When the cancer came, he couldn't manage it anymore. He wanted to devote himself to the cancer. Or maybe the cancer made it worse. I don't remember."

"But what do you remember?"

She lets go of my hand, walks away from me. She sits down on the couch. I follow her and sit down next to her, close. Our sofa is nothing like the one in the Coles' den, the leather one with buttons all over that creaked when I moved on it. Ours is plush and soft, cozy, with extra pillows bunched in the corners—a feminine couch. For the first time, I realize that ours is a house where only women have lived—that Jeremy has spent more time here than any other man, and I wonder why his maleness never felt invasive here. Just stepping inside this apartment, you'd know it was the home of a girl who didn't have a father.

My mother continues, slowly. "He was taking so many pills. I didn't notice, because there were so many others. He was always taking pills; I assumed he was taking all of his pills."

"What kind of pills did he stop taking?"

"Antidepressants," she whispers.

"He was depressed?"

"Yes, but he managed it."

"And then he didn't?"

"And then he didn't. I thought he was just, well, sad because of the cancer. I thought that was normal; I thought he and his doctors were taking care of everything, managing both. And he was a doctor. I always trusted him to know what was best, because he'd always been so responsible about it in the past, so determined to be well and have this life that we were making. He even gave me some antianxiety pills because I was so tense over the cancer. I wondered, later, if he did that so I could keep calm—" She pauses, and she doesn't finish the sentence. She's crying hard now and I want to cry too, but I try not to let that show because I'm worried that if I reveal any weakness, she'll stop telling me.

"We put him back on the pills, the antidepressants, as soon as I found out. I insisted and I trusted him, but maybe he wasn't taking them, or maybe he started and they made it worse. I was sure all those pills would fix everything. They'd always worked before."

I think I understand, but I need to say it out loud.

"He killed himself."

She nods. Her head moves so shakily, I think it will fall off her neck.

"By taking pills."

"Yes."

"How did he get them?"

She laughs, and it comes out like a cackle. "Sweetheart, that man had more pills than a Duane Reade. He had access to pills; he had extra pills; he was never at a loss for pills. His life had been run by pills since before I knew him—pills to control the depression, pills for migraines, pills to sleep at night." It occurs to me that I inherited my migraines from him. I'd always assumed it, since my mother doesn't get them, but she'd never said anything.

"Jesus Christ," she adds angrily, standing up now to pace. "He was a bloody anesthesiologist. He knew exactly how to overdose. He'd made a career out of preventing overdoses." I never knew what kind of doctor he was. No wonder his oncologist remembered him; even if they hadn't worked together, this is, like Jeremy said he said, the kind of story you don't forget.

"And you didn't want me to know."

"Of course not. Oh God, when you were in first grade, do you remember, you asked me why you didn't have a daddy. I couldn't, I couldn't tell you. I didn't want you to think he left you like that."

"It was third grade," I say quietly.

"It would have been the only thing you remembered him for."

"You didn't give me anything else to remember!" I shout, standing up too now. "I pretended my parents were divorced ever since then—since that day in third grade. I told everyone he left us to move to Arizona."

She looks shocked, like it never occurred to her that *not* knowing made me different, made me have to create some better story, some easier explanation.

"You never told me stories about him, never told me about the things that we did together before he died. Maybe I could have had some memories if you'd helped me."

She doesn't say anything. I keep digging for information. "And so no one outside the family knew, then. Everyone figured it was the cancer."

"Yes. In that case, the cancer was a convenience."

"I'm glad it was convenient for you," I say, and I hate how nasty I sound.

She looks straight at me now, and her expression is devastating. I immediately regret being cruel, having shouted. "You said you were old enough now," she says softly. "You said you could take it. No one outside the family knows, and no one should. This is a"— she chokes on the word—"a *private* matter."

I nod. "Yes, Mom, it is a private matter, a matter for family. But I'm just as much a part of this family as you are, and you didn't trust me with it."

"Well, you have it now. What are you going to do with it?" She looks frightened.

This question stops me cold. I'd been so concerned with getting the facts that I never gave any thought to what I'd do once I had them. I sit back down on the couch, lowering myself onto it without turning to look and make sure it's there. "I don't know. I'm just—I'm going to live with it. I'm going to figure out how you live with it."

She nods.

I look up at her and ask: "How have you lived with it?"

She sits down next to me.

"It's not as hard as you think," she exhales. "You just . . . get used to it."

"I've been used to living without a father for a long time."

"Yes, but now you have to be used to living with a father who took himself away from you."

As if she can hear me thinking the word "abandon," my mother shakes her head.

"I was mad at him for so long. He knew what he was doing. He put his affairs in order and made sure that you and I were taken

care of. It was his idea that I sell our townhouse. I remember thinking he was nuts to want to move when he was still sick, but he did,
and so I said okay. After he died, I figured out what he was doing:
he'd wanted me to have the money; he knew we wouldn't need
such a big place; I think he even knew me well enough to know
that I'd want to move in with my mother. He set up a trust for you,
for me—everything. I was so mad at him for that."

"Why?"

"At least if he'd left things a mess, I could have believed that
he'd lost control somehow. But he planned it all perfectly, just like
he did everything else." She presses her hair back from her forehead.
Her eyes are very bright, but she keeps talking to me. "Connelly,
you know, I just loved him so much. I thought I made him happy.
I hated being apart from him even for a day—I always wanted to
be near him. I thought he felt the same way about us. I was so mad
that you and I weren't enough for him to live for."

She sighs; traces her lips with her finger, thinking; and her voice
is different, softer, when she continues. "But eventually you stop
being mad; eventually you realize that being mad is worse than
what he did. Eventually you understand that he tried his best to
live and he couldn't."

I'm not entirely sure she believes what she's saying. It sounds
too much like something you'd read in a book about how to get
over your husband's suicide. And I can't help noticing that it's ironic
that I invented a father who abandoned us, because she was scared
that if I knew the truth, I would always think that my father did
abandon us.

"But I didn't think you could understand. You're still so

178

young, and you didn't know him like I did. And I just didn't want you to think that your father didn't love us, didn't love you, enough."

"I don't think that."

"Not yet." She exhales slowly. "But you will. You'll be angry soon, just like I was. But when you are angry, I want you to remember what I'm about to tell you: He loved you more than anything. This thing inside him killed him the same as the cancer might have. If he could have survived it, he would have." This time, I know she means what she's saying, and I believe her. I know that she's right; I know that she's telling the truth.

And then she hugs me, tight. I can't remember the last time we hugged like this, but I must have been younger, because now I notice that my mother is small—smaller, in fact, than I am. I can feel how skinny she is: I can feel the bones in her arms and hands pressing hard around my ribs. She holds me so tight that it hurts, but I don't mind. Instead, I wonder that someone this thin and this small can be so strong. And I do feel—if only for a second—anger at the man who left her alone, who left us alone together. I recognize that this small piece of anger has just found its way inside my body, where it will dig in under my skin and try to grow stronger. I know that whether or not it was the right thing to do, my mother wanted to protect me from this anger. But I feel ready to begin the work of overcoming it.

When she releases her grasp and looks at me, she holds my hands. And I wonder if she and my father had liked holding hands, or if they were one of those couples that would never do that in public. And now I know that I will ask her someday.

She hugs me again before we retreat into our rooms, the opposite ends of the apartment that maybe don't seem so far apart now. I take off the clothes from the funeral, taking care to put everything back in its place. It's only four in the afternoon, but I'm getting ready for bed. I think this is the most tired I have ever been in my entire life. When I climb into bed, the sheets are smooth and I fall asleep fast. I wake up later to the ringing of the phone, and I know that Jeremy is waiting for me downstairs.

"Were you sleeping?" he asks as I step off the elevator.

I nod. "I've been sleeping all day."

"I'm jealous. I'm so tired, but there are all these people at our house, all waiting to talk to me or feed me or see if I need anything. I thought everyone would be gone by now, but there's a bunch of guys smoking cigars in my father's study. I had to sneak out."

"I can't imagine how tough this day was for you."

Jeremy nods and then he grins, one of his crazy big smiles. "We got lost on the way to the cemetery."

"What?" I ask, beginning to laugh.

"In that hearse, with Kate in the back—I swear to God, all of a sudden we were driving down past all these cookie-cutter houses. The driver just kept going because he didn't want us to know he was lost. Then all of a sudden he pulled into one of the driveways— you know, to turn around. That kinda gave it away, finally."

"That's really funny," I say, covering my mouth.

"I know; my parents and I were laughing so hard, you wouldn't believe it. Felt like Kate was playing a trick on us."

"Maybe she just wanted you to remember something funny about today."

Jeremy nods. "Yeah, I bet she did."

"I bet she did," I echo.

Jeremy shifts his gaze beyond me, out onto Madison Avenue, and smiles faintly. I smile too. I know we're both thinking about Kate. Being without her still feels new, and strange.

Jeremy lights a couple of cigarettes, and we both take long drags.

Jeremy exhales. "Did you do it?"

"I did."

He smiles at me. "Good."

He doesn't ask me for more, and I don't want to tell him yet. I'm not ready to tell him yet. I know my mother wouldn't want me to, and I'll respect her wishes for now. I know I will tell him. But not tonight; maybe not for a long time.

"How do you feel?" he asks.

I think for a moment. My body is finally completely calm. The itching has stopped and my skin feels soft under my clothes. It occurs to me that this is the most princess-y thing ever to happen to me; not Rapunzel, a peasant girl locked in her tower, but Sleeping Beauty in the woods, a princess from a different kingdom. They tried to protect her by raising her without letting her know who or what she was. And then one day, maybe because of a boy she met in the forest, she's told that she's royal, but that hers was a tragic and dangerous beginning, a tightly kept secret. But still, she returns to the palace to live the life she was born for—which, as it happens, totally plunges her into that world of danger from which they'd been trying to protect her all those years. If only she'd always known the whole story: maybe then, she wouldn't have pricked her finger on that spindle after all. Or, at least, she'd have known what to expect when she did.

And so I feel, for once, like a princess.

I answer Jeremy: "Different."

He nods. "How do you feel?" I ask.

He smiles down at me, tosses his cigarette on the ground, and puts his arm around me. "Different."

I toss my cigarette next to his and stamp them both out.

"And cold," I add, relaxing in his hold.

"Me too. Only a few more months and we'll be smoking in the springtime."

I smile and lean against him. I feel warm.

> But we were never lonely and never afraid
> when we were together.
> —Ernest Hemingway
> *A Farewell to Arms*

ACKNOWLEDGMENTS

To my friends and colleagues at Random House Children's Books: Thank you very much for supporting this book.

Thanks to Erin Clarke for her constant guidance and encouragement; for knowing what needed to be said, as well as what was better left unsaid. Thanks to Nancy Hinkel and the entire Knopf editorial team. My thanks to Chip Gibson for his support, sense of humor, and unending kindness. Thanks to Kate Gartner and Isabel Warren-Lynch for the beautiful cover. Many, many thanks to my friends in marketing and publicity. And, to my family in retail and consumer marketing: Thank you for being a splendid place to call home.

My endless appreciation to Sarah Burnes for her unyielding optimism, patience, and editorial savvy. Thanks to everyone at the Gernert Company, especially Courtney Gatewood.

I have been very lucky to have had magnificent teachers—at P.S. 24, Spence, and Barnard—as well as lucky to have read extraordinary writers, whose work has made my life infinitely better. Thank you for encouraging me to write and, moreover, for teaching me to read. Thanks especially to Mary Gordon and Caz Phillips.

Thanks to my marvelous group of friends and my extended

family—and a special thank-you to those of you who were indulgent enough to read early drafts of this manuscript, and patient enough to tell me which title you liked best (over and over again!). Your advice helped shape this story into the book it finally became. Thank you to Tina Dubois Wexler, Joanne Brownstein, Rachel Feld (mentor, cheerleader, friend), Jessica DePaul, Ruth Homberg, John Adamo. Thanks also to Roya, Arielle, Noreen, Jen, Mindy, Ranse, Phil. Thanks to the entire Gravitt family: Janie, Brian, Laura, and John.

Much love, gratitude, and admiration to my father, Joel Sheinmel; my mother, Elaine Sheinmel; my sister, Courtney Sheinmel; and my grandmothers, Diane Buda and Doris Sheinmel.

And to my best friend and my most beloved, JP Gravitt: Every day when I wake up and you are there, it is a good day.

> My little dog—a heartbeat at my feet.
> —Edith Wharton

ABOUT THE AUTHOR

Alyssa Sheinmel was born in Stanford, California. She is a graduate of New York City's Spence School and Barnard College.

Alyssa lives in New York City and works in children's book publishing. *The Beautiful Between* is her first novel.